D1326991

TOMORROW'S TREASON

One thing marred Jon Troy's idyllic marriage: his powerful American father-in-law. Maximillian Felard, governor of a Southern state, had been accustomed to having his only daughter at his beck and call, and saw no reason why her marriage to the young British diplomat should alter things. When scandal broke over his son-in-law's head, Fel was eager to hush it up in exchange for hustling Jon out of Washington – and making him agree to a divorce.

When next the two met it was at an ecology conference in Norway, where Fel judged it politically timely to make his interest in the subject known, and Jon was reluctantly shepherding the British delegation. To his astonishment, Jon discovered the Communist-hating Fel in secret communication with a beautiful East German delegate. When Fel was suddenly incapacitated, Jon put his own career at risk.

He found himself trapped in a network of violence and double dealing in which personal lives and political pressures were hopelessly intertwined. If treason was planned for tomorrow, tomorrow was already here.

Also by
PALMA HARCOURT

*

A SLEEP OF SPIES
AGENTS OF INFLUENCE
AT HIGH RISK
DANCE FOR DIPLOMATS
A FAIR EXCHANGE
CLIMATE FOR CONSPIRACY

TOMORROW'S TREASON

*

PALMA HARCOURT

THE
COMPANION BOOK CLUB
LONDON AND SYDNEY

THE COMPANION BOOK CLUB

The Club is not a library; all books are the pro-
perty of members. There is no entrance fee or
any payment beyond the low Club price of each
book. Details of membership will gladly be sent
on request.

Write to:
The Companion Book Club,
Odhams Books, Rushden, Northants.

Or, in Australia, write to:
The Companion Book Club,
C/- Hamlyn House Books, P.O. Box 252
Dee Why, N.S.W. 2099

---

*Made and printed in Great Britain
for the Companion Book Club
by Morrison & Gibb Ltd, Edinburgh*
600872564
880/356

For Rennie and Hamish

Prelude

'Carol,' I said. 'For God's sake let's be sensible. Please, darling – '

We had had our share of rows in the eighteen months we had been married, and originally this one, monumental though it was, had seemed no different from the others. Like all the rest it had started over a trifle – something to do with our baby son, Paul – but there was a dreadful finality about it. I had begun to sense this and it frightened me.

Carol ignored my plea for sense. She was whey-faced and trembling, but her dominant emotion was anger as she said: 'You'd better accept it, Jon. I'm not going back to Washington with you tomorrow – or ever. Our marriage is over. Finished. Fel was right. It was a mistake. Fortunately, mistakes can be remedied.'

If, at that point, she hadn't mentioned Fel I might have done something positive: taken her in my arms, grovelled at her feet – anything not to lose her. I loved her very much. As it was, the reference to Fel rekindled my anger.

'To hell with your father!' I said.

It was a stupid thing to say and I didn't even mean it. I didn't hate Fel. In many ways I liked, respected and admired him.

Maximillian Felard, third-generation American, rich, charismatic and Governor of one of the great States of the southern USA, was a power within his Party, a figure to be reckoned with in American society and politics, and accus-

9

tomed to a life of privilege and power beyond anything I had experienced. It was understandable that when Carol, whom I had met on a skiing holiday in Canada, introduced me, he was not impressed. By his standards, a junior British diplomat was a poor catch for his only child. This was fair enough, and I could forgive him his attempts to prevent the marriage. I could even forgive him his offer to buy me off, though it made me cringe at the time. What I couldn't forgive was the Olympian way he interfered after we were married.

Because his wife had been crippled by polio twenty years before and was a semi-invalid, Carol had acted as her father's hostess and shared his social burdens since she was fifteen or sixteen. Fel appeared to see no reason why this shouldn't continue. In spite of the fact that we lived in Washington, he still required his daughter's presence whenever it suited him, seemingly unaware that his demands made my life with Carol impossible. He had been the cause of row after row between us. When I said, 'To hell with him!' I felt I had some cause.

Carol ignored my curses. 'Goodbye, Jon,' she said, and each word was ice-covered.

Her head held high, she turned and walked from the room, shutting the door decisively behind her, leaving me – angry and hurt and disbelieving – to stare at its blank white panels. My reactions were slow. By the time I had gathered my wits and gone after her, she was disappearing into her mother's suite, and I couldn't follow her there. Fel himself wouldn't have intruded upon his wife at seven o'clock in the evening when, with the help of her maid, she was dressing. Carol alone was privileged.

The thought of Mary Felard struggling into her elegant clothes reminded me of the official reception for which she was making such an effort. Perhaps she needed to attend. I didn't. I was on leave, and Fel was my father-in-law, not my ambassador. Pulling off my black tie, I went through into the bedroom. In three minutes I had changed from dinner-jacket to lounge suit.

I'm not sure what I had in mind. All I wanted at that moment was to get away from the Governor's Mansion, to go somewhere I didn't feel smothered by Fel. If Carol didn't consider it more important to be my wife than Fel's daughter, then our marriage was really over . . .

I was half-way down the imposing staircase when I saw Bob Verson at the bottom.

'Where are you off to, Jon?' His eyes travelled from my suede shoes to my crimson tie.

'Out.'

He smiled. I didn't like his smile, but then I didn't like Robert F. Verson. The F stood for Felard, and he was a distant cousin of Fel's, as well as being his Executive Assistant. And the dislike was mutual; he had hoped to marry Carol.

'You're not honouring us with your presence at the dinner tonight?'

'No. You can remove my place at the table.'

His smile widened, but he wasn't amused. 'Had another spat with Carol?'

The pseudo-sympathetic manner that larded his obvious familiarity with my private life infuriated me. I slammed out of the house. I had flown down from Washington so I didn't have my own car, but there was always a selection in the garage. I took the white Cadillac because it was the nearest. Opening the windows to allow the warm September wind to blow through, I headed for the town, the bars and whatever other attractions the State capital might offer.

Later in the evening, bored, lonely and miserable, I went to the cinema. I stared at the screen. The film was good but I couldn't enjoy it. The background noises, the whispering, the crackling of candy papers and the crunching of soft-drink

11

cartons became increasingly more irritating. My seat was uncomfortable. I decided to leave.

It was now that I became aware of the girl – or rather her scent. The scent was French, very expensive and to me very familiar; it was Carol's favourite. As I passed them – she and her companion were sitting in the back row and must have come in after me – the scent triumphed even over the sickly smell of popcorn that permeated the whole cinema. I looked at them with mild interest. The girl had bent down and I had only a fleeting impression of blonde hair and a blue coat. I took in more of her companion. He was a square, swarthy man in a green jacket. I had never seen him before and it might have been the dim light, but his eyes, meeting mine, seemed to shine with curiosity, his mouth to thin into a smile as if he recognized me. It was vaguely disturbing.

Five minutes later I had forgotten them. I went into a bar and ordered a highball. When it arrived I drank deeply. I almost relaxed. Then I smelt the scent, Carol's scent.

The girl had come into the bar. She was by herself, attractive and with fair hair, not natural like Carol's but not brassy, and a thin, intelligent face. She was carrying her coat over her arm, an inexpensive coat that didn't match the French perfume. As she slipped on to the stool beside me she dropped her handbag. I picked it up for her.

'Thanks. That was real kind of you.' She had a pleasant husky voice.

The barman approached. 'And what will the lady have?'

She looked at my glass, shook her head and said: 'Not a highball. A Manhattan?'

It was a neat pick-up, but I didn't mind. 'My pleasure,' I said, amused. At least she was a distraction.

Her cocktail came and I paid for it. She thanked me profusely, and assured me she wasn't in the habit of letting strange men buy her drinks in bars. Oddly enough I believed her. I wondered what she had done with her boy-friend.

'My name's Jon Troy,' I said. 'What do you call yourself?'

'Darlene . . . Darlene Smith.'

'A pretty name.'

We chatted idly. I told her about my various posts and she said she had always wanted to travel, but she wasn't really interested. There was a nervousness to her, an edginess, and her eyes flicked constantly round the room.

Suddenly she made a big play of noticing the time. 'Gee, I didn't realize it was so late. I – I suppose – it's awful to ask you, but I'd be terribly grateful – I mean, you did say you were living out the west side of town . . .'

'You'd like a lift home?'

'Oh, I wouldn't want to take you out of your way. But if you're going down the Parkway you could drop me. I'll show you. And thanks a million, Mr Troy.'

She had taken my question as an offer, which wasn't exactly what I had intended. But she was standing up, gesturing to me to help her into her coat. I could scarcely refuse.

I told myself to be careful. In spite of her apparent naïveté and the triteness of her words, she had manœuvred me very neatly. Why? I thought that perhaps I could guess.

I was to drive her home, be persuaded to go in for a night-cap and subsequently be found by an irate husband – the character who had been with her in the movie – in her bed. To the question 'Why me?', the answer was either chance or recognition. If they knew me by sight they could easily have decided in the cinema that the Governor's son-in-law would make an excellent mark.

I smiled grimly. If that was their game, they were going to be disappointed.

The girl seemed unaware of my silence. She was busy telling me about the clients at the beauty salon where she worked. I started the car and drove fast out of the town centre and along the Parkway.

13

'Where do you want to be dropped?'

My question was abrupt and stopped her in mid-sentence. She laughed nervously, fidgeted with her hair.

'Not far. About half a mile. Okay?'

'Of course.' I glanced at the speedometer. 'And that will be all right for you?'

'Fine.'

I had given her the opportunity to ask for a lift to her door, but she hadn't taken it. And before the half-mile was up she was telling me to slow. I drew in to the side of the road, some yards beyond a street lamp.

'Here we are,' she said. 'Thanks, Mr Troy. For the ride, and for the drinks. Don't bother to get out.'

Amused at myself for the suspicions I had been harbouring against poor Darlene, I leaned across her to open the door. It was then I heard a sound behind me.

I had a second of attention, of fear. Someone could have slipped into the back of the Cadillac while I was at the cinema and waited his chance to mug me. I hadn't checked. Darlene had been chattering, distracting.

The next moment I felt a prick in the side of my neck, stinging, like a mosquito bite. I flung my hand up to the place. Somehow it never got there. My arm had grown unbelievably heavy. My fingers slipped across my cheek, my mouth, and my hand dropped back into my lap.

The pain in my neck was excruciating. It paralysed me. Waves of darkness closed over me and I fell, faster and faster, through black space, turning over as I fell . . .

Time elapsed, twenty minutes, half an hour. I don't know. Mostly it was a blank. Otherwise it was a series of questions. Was my mouth being forced open? Was something burning my throat? Were fingernails, sharp as claws, raking my cheek? Was someone ripping my clothes? The whole thing was a nightmare.

14

Eventually I woke. What I saw and felt and experienced was no dream. But it still had all the qualities of nightmare.

I was lying on my back by the side of the road. The pavement was hard under me. My shirt was torn. My jacket seemed to have disappeared. I was cold. My face hurt, and the corner of my mouth. There was a lot of activity going on, people, cars. Carefully I lifted my head.

The Cadillac, Fel's Cadillac, stood at right angles in front of me, its nose buried in a wall. There was broken glass and metal scattered around it. Beyond were a police car and an ambulance. And suddenly I became aware of a high-pitched hysterical sobbing.

I tried to sit up. At once I became dizzy and nauseated. I fell back. But I had seen a stretcher being lifted into the ambulance and, in the further shadows, a police van and what looked like another private car.

A face bent over me, grew to balloon size and exploded. I shut my eyes tight. A voice shouted: 'Hi, Sergeant! He's come to.'

There were running footsteps. A shoe kicked me in the ribs, and went on kicking me again and again. I cried out in protest, opened my eyes. Above me stood the man I had seen in the cinema, the man who had been with Darlene Smith. There was no mistaking him even though his features were contorted in rage. Beside himself with anger, he kicked me and cursed me as he kicked. It took two policemen to pull him off and, as they dragged him away, he shot a gob of spittle into my face. That revolted me.

Instinctively I started to scrub my cheek with the back of my hand, but the pain was so intense I had to stop. I felt dirty and humiliated. If I had been standing I would have hit him, cops or no cops. As it was, I was incapable of retaliating, incapable of anything. Such puny effort as I did make exhausted me. I blacked out.

Consciousness returned as I was lifted, none too gently, on

to a stretcher. The ambulance, its siren growing fainter, was disappearing into the distance. Puzzled, I made to push away some hair that had fallen into my eyes; I wanted to see what was happening. And the realization came to me that there were handcuffs on my wrists. Tentatively I moved my legs. They too were cuffed.

'What the hell's going on?' I demanded. 'Where are you taking me? What's this all about?'

No one paid any attention. My stretcher was picked up, carried to the police van and thrust into the back. The world reeled around me.

My next clear memory was waking in a prison cell. I was lying on a hard bed attached to a wall. Gingerly I sat up. I felt light-headed and bloody awful. But I could stand, even walk. I was more or less back to normal.

There was a sound of footsteps, the clang of keys and the cell door was flung open. Two policemen came in. One was carrying a breakfast tray; I could smell coffee, bacon. Unexpectedly I was hungry. The other had an overnight bag, towel, soap, shaving mirror, my jacket.

'Mr Troy,' the older of the two men said, ignoring my spate of questions. 'I am instructed to tell you that Mr Verson will be here to see you later.'

Relief overwhelmed me. Bob Verson would sort everything out. Verson, much as I disliked him, was a capable guy. He would know what to do, and how best to do it. He could tell the fuzz where they got off, get me out of this bloody cell, arrange whatever had to be arranged.

In silence I waited for the cops to go. Then I opened the bag. It contained a change of underwear, suit, shirt, tie, socks, shoes and razor – all mine. Verson must have gone to some trouble to collect them. Against my will I felt a rush of gratitude for him. At least now I could make myself presentable.

16

I had a pee and washed my hands at the basin. The water was hot and I promised myself a proper wash later. Breakfast had priority. I started with the coffee, which was good but made my mouth hurt. Somehow my appetite faded and I had to force myself to eat.

Afterwards I tried to shave, an impossible task as one glance in the mirror assured me. I was a horrific sight. My left cheek had been savagely raked, the lines marked by half-clotted blood, and the corner of my mouth was torn. It looked bad enough to need stitching. Shaken by my appearance, I dressed and lay on the cot, trying to remember.

Time passed. I thought of Carol, and what Fel would have to say about the trouble I had got myself into, and the girl Darlene, and the need to be back in Washington by Monday morning whatever happened. Repeatedly I caught myself casting quick glances at my watch.

And at last Bob Verson arrived.

'Bob! Am I glad to see you.'

'I wish I could say it was mutual.'

His scorn was like a slap in the face. I stared at him. Verson was usually the typical clean-cut, well-pressed, efficient Ivy Leaguer, but today for once he appeared a little jaded, his Brooks Brothers suit a trifle crumpled, his efficiency slightly nerve-ridden. Obviously he was short on sleep and that would be my fault. I couldn't expect him to be pleased about it.

'I'm sorry, truly sorry,' I said. 'I realize I'm being a hell of a nuisance, but it was an accident. I must have blacked out – '

'Accident? Blacked out? You're crazy. Nobody but nobody's going to believe that.' He sat himself down at the table and opened his briefcase.

'It's the truth, Bob. I don't remember a thing after I stopped the car on the Parkway.'

'You don't remember Mrs Smith?' His sarcasm was heavy.

'Mrs Smith? You mean Darlene? Yes, of course I remem-

17

ber her. I bought her a drink in a bar and she asked me to give her a lift. How is she? Is she badly hurt?'

Verson was arranging papers in front of him as if he were a lawyer, and for answer he picked out a photograph and handed it to me. It was a close-up of a woman lying in what appeared to be a hospital bed, her face so battered that at first I didn't recognize her.

'Oh Christ!' I said. 'Poor Darlene.'

His temper flared, startling me. 'You goddam Limey hypocrite! You rape the girl and then you have the nerve to say –'

'I raped the girl?' I said in horrified disbelief, the words without meaning.

'You sure as hell did. And don't tell me you've forgotten, Jon. Dear Jesus, when I think you ever touched Carol, I – I –'

Suddenly my anger matched his. 'Now listen, Verson, I may have had a blackout but I'm damned if I raped Darlene Smith, or anyone else.'

'No, you listen! And stop being a smart-ass.' He banged his hand down on the table. 'There's enough circumstantial evidence to hang you twice over. I've got it all here. The depositions. From Mr Smith. From Mrs Smith. From the bartender, the police, the ambulance men – the hospital. You were drunk as a coot and you raped her. The doc will swear to it. She was raped, brutally raped.'

'But not by me!'

'That's what you say, Jon, but you're wasting your time. Why don't you quit acting the innocent? Nobody's going to believe you.'

'The Smiths must have framed me,' I said, hearing the doubt in my own voice.

Verson laughed mirthlessly. 'Why should they do that? Give me one good reason. Smith's no bum. He's a merchant, a businessman respected in the town. He's got a store on the corner of Donaldson and Fifth, a gents' outfitters that brings him in a tidy income. And Darlene, his wife, she works in a beauty salon. She's a real nice lady. No, you'll never make that one stick.' He passed me the statements. 'Read these.'

I glanced through them. I couldn't bring myself to concentrate. My mind was in a turmoil. Darlene had lied to me, but they were only petty lies, easily explained by her admission that she had quarrelled with her husband at the cinema and gone to the bar to annoy him. Once there, she said, she had regretted her impulse. She had been thankful to recognize the Governor's son-in-law and accept a lift home. But she hadn't reached home.

It was a plausible story, seemingly impossible to refute, as it was impossible to refute the fact that Darlene had been raped. But why had she accused me? Why? Why? I remembered the paralysing pain in my neck, the fall into nothingness. Had the same thing happened to her? Did she really believe it was I who had raped her?

'What about the accident?' I asked. 'How's that meant to have happened?'

'Don't you know, Jon? Mrs Smith thinks she must have regained consciousness after the assault and, terrified out of her wits as to what you intended next, started to fight you while you were driving.' Verson shrugged. 'Incidentally, the penalty for rape in this State can be up to twenty years, and it wouldn't be in a fancy gaol like this one. You wouldn't survive, Jon. You'd rot to death.' He grinned at me, showing his beautifully capped teeth. 'Personally that wouldn't grieve me one bit, but Fel has decreed otherwise.'

'What do you mean?' I was stupefied.

'Fel, as you know, is State Governor here, and a very powerful man. To oblige him the Smiths are prepared to take an all-expense-paid vacation that ought to make Darlene as good as new again. In return, they won't press charges against Fel's son-in-law. If there are any questions – not that there will be, because the police sergeant's an astute man and, once he'd looked in your wallet, he only booked you for

19

drunken driving and anyway the head fuzz is a buddy of Fel's – but if there are any questions, Darlene will swear you were knocked out and she's no idea who screwed her.'

'But that's absurd! Bloody absurd! I'm not guilty of anything. I don't need Fel to bribe a lot of people to tell a lot of lies for my sake. What I want is a thorough investigation and – '

'What you want, Jon, doesn't matter a good goddam. You'd better understand that right away,' Verson said viciously. 'It's what Fel wants that counts, and after what you've done he wants you out of his State, out of his life and out of Carol's life for good. I've got your weekend bag in my automobile. The rest of your things will be sent on later. I'm to drive you to the airport and Fel's pilot will fly you to Washington. And that will be that. You won't have to worry. Fel will fix everything at this end. All you have to do is sign a letter to Carol and thank your stars you're getting off so lightly.'

'No!' I said. 'For the umpteenth time I'm telling you. I haven't done anything. I'm not guilty and I'm not running away. I'm not leaving Carol. I don't care a damn what Fel or – '

'Cool it!' Verson stood up. 'Jon, you have two alternatives. If you fight you'll lose everything. Be in no doubt about that. Every bit of evidence is against you. Diplomat or not, without Fel's help you'll go to gaol for a very long time. However, if you're smart there'll be no scandal, either for the Felards – and at least you must care about Carol – or for your own family in England; don't forget them. And your career will be safe. That's important to you, isn't it?'

He paused and eyed me warily. 'Either way Carol's going to divorce you, as she informed you last night. You realize that, don't you? And she'll never let you have custody of Paul, not after this – this business. She'd rather – '

'You mean she knows. You told her, and she believes – '

'She was with Fel and me when the cops phoned. She demanded to see whatever evidence I found. Fel agreed she should. It was her right. So naturally she doesn't want to see or hear from you ever again. She's – she's revolted, as any decent girl would be.'

'And she's condemned me out of hand, without even hearing what I've got to say?' I was bitter. 'God rot all the Felards!'

Verson shrugged. He had finished collecting his papers and had shut his briefcase. 'I'll be back in a half-hour for your decision.'

Thirty minutes later I signed the letter which was to provide Carol with grounds for divorce. It said that our marriage was at an end, I was leaving her for a girl-friend in Washington, and I gave up all claim to my son Paul. I had never despised myself as much as I did at that moment, but as far as I could see I had no choice.

PART ONE

Chapter One

'JON, H.E. WANTS YOU – on the double.'

'What for? What have I done?'

I was only half joking. The British Ambassador to Norway was a courteous man and not in the habit of issuing such abrupt summonses. His secretary, her dark head poked around my office door, grinned at me.

'Your guilty conscience should tell you that,' she said.

'You did mean on the double, though?' I looked reluctantly at my paper-strewn desk. I had almost completed the up-dating of a brief on NATO's vulnerability along the Norwegian–Finnish border. Half an hour would see me through. 'He's waiting for me?'

'He is indeed.' She was serious. 'Come on, Jon. He wants you now – not next month.'

I followed her along the corridor and up the broad stairs, admiring her neat buttocks and slim legs. I liked Jane Hamlin and, because we were both unattached – my divorce from Carol had celebrated its second anniversary – and lived in the same block of flats overlooking Oslofjord, we saw a good deal of each other. Our friendship, however, was strictly platonic. Personally I intended it should remain so. I didn't kid myself. I knew I was still in love with my ex-wife. And anyway, in my opinion office romances were to be avoided.

Jane knocked at the door. 'Mr Troy's here, Sir William.'

'Thank you. Come in, Jon, and sit you down.' H.E.,

having finished scribbling a note on his memo pad, regarded me through heavy-rimmed spectacles. He came at once to the point. 'We've just had the sad news that Duncan's mother has died. I sent him off to Fornebu immediately. If the London plane's on time he should be home tonight. But he won't be back for a week and, what with leave and summer flu, we're already short of staff, which means I've no one else to send to Lysebu – to the World Environment Conference – except you, Jon.'

'But, sir – ' I protested. 'I don't know the first thing about it.'

'My dear boy, you must know something – enough to make appropriate noises.' He smiled wryly. 'Everyone does. You can't open a newspaper or turn on the radio these days without being bludgeoned by ecological threats. According to the environmentalists we'll all be nose deep in our own ordure unless we take action, today or tomorrow – a sorry state of affairs, I must admit.'

'You don't think it's a very serious problem, sir.'

'Oh yes, I do, Jon. But I also think it's a popular bandwagon and a lot of people riding on it don't care a damn about the real issues. They're only using the topic as a means to an end, their end, whatever their end may be. However, that's not our concern. Our business is to see that everything goes smoothly for the UK delegation and that none of them gets into trouble.'

'What sort of trouble?'

'Any sort. This is a big international conference. The delegates are from all over the world, including the communist countries, and they're a mixed bag – politicians, civil servants, academics, businessmen – and -women. Personally, I'm not sure the Norwegians have the facilities for organizing something of this size. It may be a bit of a shambles. Anyway, Jon, your job is to act as nanny to the Brits, keep them happy and keep their noses clean, but try not to be too obvious about it. Jane will give you the details, lists of meetings, potted biographies and so on. You'll be staying at Lysebu, of course. Well – any questions?'

Several leapt to mind. A week at a conference centre some forty minutes' drive from Oslo was going to play havoc with my social life. It was no use objecting to that. H.E. wouldn't be sympathetic. The rest Jane could answer, with one exception.

'Sir, I'm due to go on leave on Monday week. Will it affect that?'

'No, I don't see why it should. It's a week's meeting. Delegates register tomorrow and Sunday, welcoming dinner with speeches Sunday night, final meeting the following Saturday morning. Then you'll be free.' He sighed. 'I only hope Duncan will be back before you go.'

So did I. It wasn't that I had planned anything special for my leave, and considering how undemanding the Oslo post was – at least compared with Washington – I couldn't plead overwork, but I didn't want my holiday cancelled. I was looking forward to getting away for a while.

'Thank you, sir.'

H.E. nodded his dismissal and I made for Jane's office. She had a stack of material ready for me. I leafed through it. There was a map of the conference centre; apparently it consisted of a group of wooden buildings linked by covered walkways or, in one case, by an underground tunnel. The centre was large and sprawling; delegates were sure to get lost. There was a list of meetings with brief notes attached. Phrases like 'oil pollution', 'melting of the ice-cap', 'reclamation of the desert' and 'aller vert' caught my eyes. I groaned.

Jane laughed. 'Cheer up. It mayn't be so bad. I expect the place will be swarming with smashing Norwegian girls.'

'Yes.' The thought didn't cheer me; I had visions of randy delegates chasing beautiful blondes along the corridors, and wondered if this was included in the 'trouble' H.E. had

27

mentioned. I hoped the Brits would be a dull lot. 'When do I have to be at Lysebu?'

'Tomorrow afternoon. It's understood that everyone's responsible for getting themselves to the centre, and most of them will be flying into Fornebu on the Sunday. Some of the Europeans will come by car, and others may find it convenient to arrive on Saturday. So, in case any of our people are early birds, you must be there.'

'Okay. I'm resigned.'

While Jane produced information, helpful hints and down-right scandal about the members of the UK delegation, I continued to glance through the bumph. The list of delegates was in alphabetical order. I ran my eye down it. Several of the names were familiar, amongst them that of Boris Gronski, a Russian whom I knew from my Washington days to be a member of the KGB and a most improbable environmentalist. I turned to the speakers.

'Jon! Jon, what is it?'

'Nothing. Why?'

My weak smile didn't disguise the lie and Jane, who knew me pretty well, was a perceptive girl. She gave me a hard look. 'My dear, didn't H.E. . . .'

'You mean, didn't H.E. say that one of the main speakers at the World Environment Conference is to be Maximillian Felard, my ex-father-in-law? No, Jane, he didn't.' I smiled ruefully. 'It was a bit of a surprise, I admit, but not important. Fel and I are on quite good terms. He writes to me every Christmas.'

This was literally true. Each December I received a reel of film and a packet of still photographs of my son, Paul. The captions were in Fel's handwriting. A brief note, typewritten but signed by the great man, gave me news of the boy – never wildly exciting – and sent formal good wishes. Carol was not mentioned.

I don't know why Fel bothered. I didn't acknowledge the

correspondence. But maybe it had done something to soften my original bitterness. Certainly I bore him no grudge.

During the intervening years I had had plenty of time to think about the night I was supposed to have raped Darlene Smith, and I could accept by now that according to his lights Fel hadn't acted unreasonably. He had given priority to his daughter and grandson and, not unnaturally for a politician, to the immaculate name of Felard. He had also saved me, albeit incidentally, from a scandal that would have ruined my career, possibly from a long prison sentence. The more I had reviewed the circumstantial evidence against me, the more I had realized how damning it was.

And so I had done nothing. Perhaps I had been wrong. Perhaps I should have made an effort to establish my innocence. But, back in Washington, I had seen no way of proving that the Smiths – respectable as they appeared to be – had set me up. Even if I could have obtained proof, it wouldn't have been much use. I couldn't have prosecuted them. The publicity would have exposed Fel's machinations on my behalf.

Admittedly I would have appreciated an apology from Fel, not least for his curt reply to the long, anguished letter I had sent him immediately after the event. I would have enjoyed spitting in Bob Verson's eye, too, making him grovel. But what had really influenced me was Carol's behaviour. She had made no attempt to communicate with me – except through her lawyers – and it seemed never to have occurred to her that possibly, just possibly, I might not be guilty. It was something I couldn't forgive her.

Suddenly aware that Jane was regarding me with sympathy I collected the material she had provided. 'I'll go and do my homework then,' I said. 'Thanks for all this, Jane.'

'My pleasure, Jon.' She smiled at me, rather sadly. 'Have a good conference.'

*　　　*　　　*

The following afternoon I set off for Lysebu. It was a hot, sultry day and I left Oslo reluctantly. Traffic was heavy, my mood sombre. I drove fast and irritably. But once I had climbed into the pine-covered mountains behind the city my spirits lightened. The conference was only for a week – probably a boring week and with the added complication of Fel's presence – but after that I should be on leave. I was humming with the car radio as I turned off the main road on to the undulating driveway that led to the centre.

Rounding a corner I saw in a hollow ahead of me the main conference hall. It was easy to recognize from the pointed roof and wooden bell-tower that made it look like a church. Fascinated by the unusual appearance of the building I was accelerating to get a closer view when my attention was abruptly drawn to the right.

A small boy, his flaxen hair gleaming in the sun, was jumping up and down on the grassy slope. He was shouting desperately and pointing to an even smaller boy who, dumb with fright and seemingly unable to get off his skateboard, was careering straight into the path of my car.

Instinctively my foot jammed on the brake and I hauled the wheel round. If my seat-belt hadn't been fastened I would have gone through the windscreen. As it was the Jaguar almost stood on its nose before it skewed at right-angles across the driveway and stopped.

My heart thumping, I looked behind me. The little boy was spreadeagled on the grass, his helmet lying beside him, his skateboard some distance away. He was screaming with the full force of his lungs. I sighed with relief. If he was able to make so much noise he couldn't have suffered irreparable damage. I scrambled out of the car and ran towards him.

His brother beat me to it. He had already pulled the child to his feet and, when I arrived, was shaking him vigorously. The screaming dwindled and ceased.

'Is he all right?' I asked.

'Yes. Thank you. He's not hurt.' I had spoken in English and the boy answered in the same language. 'It's just that he's not good yet with the skateboard. He ought to be more careful.'

I nodded solemnly and started to speak, but furious hooting interrupted me. A Volvo had drawn up behind my Jag which, I admit, was blocking the driveway. A man put his head out of the window and shouted something I didn't catch.

'What?'

The boy tugged at my sleeve. 'It's the Germans. They arrived this morning and were angry because – no food. They had to go into Oslo. My mother – it wasn't her fault. She – she – '

His English broke down and a flood of Norwegian over-whelmed me. I understood only a few words, but the message was clear. These were people he disliked – probably because they had been unpleasant to his mother.

'It's okay,' I said. 'You run along. I'll cope with them.'

He gave me a grateful look, replaced the helmet on the smaller boy's head and, holding him by one hand and the skateboard in the other, left me to it. I strolled over to the Germans' car which, I saw from the sticker on the wind-screen, had been rented at the airport.

'You will move at once. We wish to pass.'

'Certainly. I'd hate to detain you,' I said coldly.

I had intended to apologize for blocking the road, but his arrogant manner annoyed me. He was a broad-shouldered, solid man with a severely chiselled face, and I thought how appropriate he would look in Nazi uniform. His companion, on the other hand, was a runtish little man, at least ten years older, with a high forehead, a receding hairline and dark, dead eyes. He was infinitely more polite – and infinitely more frightening.

'If you would move, we would be pleased,' he said.

31

'You are an American?' It was a different voice.

Because of the direction of the sun the rear seat of the Volvo was in shadow. I had been aware of someone sitting there, but not that it was a girl. As she leaned forward the light fell on her long, pale red hair, her creamy skin and her wide, green eyes. I didn't try to hide my admiration.

'No,' I said. 'No. I'm English, Fräulein.'

'Ah!' To my chagrin she had lost interest. 'Please move your automobile.'

I didn't argue. After all, they were in the right. I was causing an obstruction. I gave the girl my best smile, ignored the two men and went to rescue my Jag. The skateboarders had disappeared.

I parked in an almost empty carpark, keeping a tactful distance from the Volvo. I didn't hurry. Purposely I let the Germans get well ahead of me and, by the time I reached the reception hall, they were nowhere to be seen. There was only a pretty blonde – one of Jane's smashing Norwegian girls – behind the desk.

I told her my name, said that I was from the British Embassy in Oslo, explained why I was replacing Duncan. As soon as she understood she smiled radiantly.

'I am sorry about your friend, Mr Troy, but you are most welcome. Please to sign the register.'

The book lay open on the counter. I signed and, curious to know if any of the UK delegates had arrived before me, turned to the previous page. Happily none had; it meant I wasn't falling down on my job and, with luck, might have the evening to myself.

In fact, I was amongst the first arrivals at the conference, though not the very first. That place had gone to Werner Günther, Erich Horst and Anna Mecklen, the trio I had met on the driveway. And I had been wrong about one thing. I was unlikely to see the big, military-type German – whether he was Günther or Horst I didn't know – in Nazi uniform.

After each of their names, in the column reserved for nationality, were the letters DDR. The three of them were East Germans, communists.

'You are in Room 121, Mr Troy. I hope you will like it. The rooms are all the same, comfortable but not lux – lux – How do you say?'

'Luxurious.'

'Thank you. Supper will be served this evening at seven. Please try to be punctual to meals. There will be wine, and always beer and soft drinks on a table in the dining-hall. You write down what you have taken. No spirits. You will get the full timetable of arrangements when you register for the conference. Registrations begin after supper tonight. I deal only with the – hotel side here, you understand?'

'I understand and it all sounds splendid. Many thanks.'

I took the room key she was offering me and bent to pick up my suitcase. On the floor beside it lay an envelope. Presumably I had knocked it off the counter while I was talking. I picked it up and made to hand it to the girl. Inadvertently I turned it over. It was addressed, in very black ink, to Mr Maximillian Felard.

'You wish to leave this for a delegate who is to come?'

'I – I – No.' I forced a smile. 'I found it on the floor. I expect someone put it on your counter when you weren't here, and I accidentally knocked it off.'

She frowned, shook her head. 'That's not possible, Mr Troy. I tidied everything when I came on duty, eight or ten minutes ago. There was no letter then and I've not left my post since.'

'Well, it's not mine, I assure you.'

She shrugged. 'No. It's not yours. Of course not. It is Mr – Mr Felard's.' She turned and slipped the envelope into a pigeon-hole marked F. She smiled at me. 'I hope you'll enjoy your conference, Mr Troy.'

I nodded my thanks, collected the suitcase and set off in

search of my room. I felt surprisingly shaken, which was absurd. If the letter had been addressed to anyone but Fel I wouldn't have thought twice about it. Annoyed with myself, I found number 121 and unlocked the door.

As I had been warned, the room was not 'lux'. The walls and ceiling were panelled pine. The floor was also wood with a couple of bright scatter mats. The bed was a long, narrow bunk made up as a couch, with a telephone on a table beside it. The rest of the furniture consisted of a built-in cupboard with shelves underneath, a desk and chair, and one moderately soft armchair. A partition hid toilet, shower and washbasin. The window was large, the curtains thin, unlined; they wouldn't keep out the light. Sardonically I wondered how some of the VIPs due to attend the conference were going to enjoy their Spartan quarters. I couldn't imagine Fel for one in these surroundings. But, as H.E. had implied, there was a lot of political mileage to be got out of the environment these days.

I unpacked, blessing Jane for reminding me to include some bottles of diplomatic Scotch in my baggage, admired the view across the valley and tried the bed. It was surprisingly comfortable. I lay there for a while, reading, and caught myself drifting off to sleep.

There were about twenty of us for supper and we divided ourselves among several small tables. I sat with the only Brits to have arrived so far, an ornithologist called Simpson-Brown and a lady soil-erosion expert. They were quiet, sensible people; it didn't take me long to realize they were unlikely to make any demands or cause me any trouble during the conference.

Reassured, I let my attention wander. At the next table Boris Gronski was talking to a couple of Canadians and snatches of their conversation reached me. They were discussing the problems involved in building on the permafrost. It was such an improbable subject to be of interest to the KGB man that I wanted to laugh.

Hastily I straightened my features. The Russian, perhaps sensing that he was being watched, had glanced in my direction. Catching my eye, he nodded his head in greeting. I smiled, nodded in return, but I was surprised. I hadn't expected Gronski to remember me.

I looked away, at the third table, where the East Germans were sitting, the girl between the two men as if they were guarding her. They were just finishing their meal and they left the dining-room before anyone else. I hoped to see them afterwards, when registration started – to be more exact, I hoped to see the fräulein – but they were nowhere around, and I resigned myself to a dull evening. While my two Brits went off for a walk, I stationed myself in the reception hall. Though I doubted that any more of my charges would arrive that day it seemed best to show willing.

Thanks again to Jane I was well equipped with paperbacks. I sat and read. The latest exposé of the latest ex-CIA man didn't completely absorb my attention. Nevertheless, I was startled when a voice from behind my chair said: 'Mr Troy. It is Mr Troy, isn't it? This is an unexpected pleasure.'

I made to stand up, dropping my book. 'Ah – Mr Gronski.'

'Don't disturb yourself, please.' Boris Gronski put his hand on my shoulder and urged me down into my seat. He perched himself on the arm of the chair beside me and lit one of the Cuban cigars he favoured. 'The pleasure was unexpected, Mr Troy, because I didn't know you were an environmentalist. Are you no longer interested in the defence business?'

To give myself a moment to think I busied myself picking up the book and marking my place. There was no reason not to tell Gronski what I was doing here but his interest puzzled me. Officially a senior Russian diplomat, he was high-ranking in the KGB, too high-ranking to waste his time on me. For that matter he was too high-ranking to be at the conference at all – unless he had a very special reason.

I explained about Duncan and, as Gronski nodded sympathetically, added: 'I must admit I was surprised to see your own name among the delegates, Mr Gronski.'

His smile widened at my remark. 'I have come only as an observer, though if necessary I am always willing to give advice – on any subject.'

He stood up and stretched himself. Five foot eight or nine, Gronski was a neat, compact man with a balding head and a pointed beard that emphasized his resemblance to Lenin. And, in his subtle way, he was just as dangerous. I would have given a lot to know what he meant by 'observer' and what kind of advice he was prepared to give – and to whom.

'Well, I mustn't keep you, Mr Troy. You'll be wanting to greet your father-in-law. I see he's just arriving.'

With a casual wave he left me, too late to make my escape. I was directly in Fel's line of vision. Probably he had already seen me. If he hadn't, Robert F. Verson certainly had. He was staring at me, his expression coldly hostile.

Verson's presence was a blow. I had steeled myself to meet Fel but, fool that I was, it hadn't occurred to me that he might bring Verson with him. I tried to encourage myself with a reminder that I had nothing to be ashamed of, but it didn't help much. Nor did it help to be aware that while I watched Verson muttering to Fel – almost certainly about me – Gronski was watching the three of us as if we were some kind of act laid on especially for his entertainment.

A different Norwegian girl was now on duty, but I saw her give Fel the letter I had found on the floor and he was slitting the envelope as he came across to me. He was a big, heavy man but light on his feet like a boxer, with a leonine head and a commanding presence. I put down my book and stood. Fel held out his hand.

'Hi, Jon. How are you?'

'All right, thank you. And you, Fel?'

'Great, just great.' He looked it too; his eyes were clear and his skin a ruddy brown. 'I heard you'd been posted to Oslo, but I didn't think "aller vert" was your line, Jon.'

'I'm standing in for a colleague.'

'Ah, good. It's nice to see you.' The gentle Southern drawl made the words seem even vaguer than they were.

Fel had taken the letter from its envelope and had started to read it. Out of the corner of my eye I watched Verson lumping their bags across the vestibule; the conference centre was run on democratic lines and service was minimal. Verson, I thought with a spurt of malice, wouldn't enjoy playing porter.

Beside me there was a sudden, choking sound. 'Jesus Christ!' Fel whispered. 'Jesus Christ!'

Beneath the tan his face was a dirty grey. He looked old, sick, and he was breathing fast through thinned nostrils. For a moment I was afraid he was having a heart attack. I caught him by the arm but angrily he shook off my hold and I realized it was the letter, now crumpled in his fist, that had been the cause of his near collapse.

'Sorry, Jon. Spot of indigestion.' He lied swiftly. He had got control of himself. 'What I need's a drink and a good night's sleep. We had a godawful flight.' He managed a savage kind of grin. He was almost back to normal, his charm breaking through. He patted me on the shoulder. 'We'll have a talk while I'm here, Jon. We must. Share our news. I promise.'

He gave me his charismatic smile and was gone. I couldn't help but admire him; Fel, in his way, was a great man. But the letter had shaken him to the roots. I had never before seen him so stripped of his carapace, so vulnerable. I found it extraordinarily disturbing, and not least because Comrade Gronski had witnessed the incident with obvious sardonic amusement.

Chapter Two

THE NEXT MORNING I woke with a sour taste in my mouth. I had drunk too much of my diplomatic Scotch the previous night, drinking alone, trying not to think about Fel – his reaction to that letter had been incredibly violent – about Carol, Darlene Smith, Verson, the whole sorry story. I pulled the duvet over my head to keep out the light and made an effort to get back to sleep. It was useless. Reluctantly I rolled out of bed.

The day was beautiful, blue sky, sunshine, already warm. I leant on the window-sill and watched a distant dot grow into a small aircraft. Nearer it looked like a big yellow bird, but as it flew down the valley the sound of its engine reverberating in the mountains spoiled the illusion. Perversely the thought of all that lovely noise-pollution cheered me up.

I showered, shaved, dressed, all in a leisurely fashion, and went down to the dining-room. I was among the last arrivals. The tables being used for breakfast were almost full and I took careful stock. Later, when the conference quota was complete, it would be possible to avoid certain delegates without making it appear too obvious. At the moment this was tricky. And it was surprising how many of them I did want to avoid – Fel, Verson, Boris Gronski, and the East Germans Horst and Günther – especially early in the morning.

Breakfast was a help-yourself meal, the food laid out on a long table at one end of the room. Ignoring the cold fish and dark brown goat's cheese, I chose a hard-boiled egg; there was a great bowl of eggs that a young Norwegian woman had just refilled. In addition I took bread, butter, marmalade and some Jarlsberg. All I needed now was coffee.

On a side table were two large copper kettles, identical in appearance, with cups and saucers beside them. I tried the nearer. It contained tea. The other produced coffee, but only dregs. I picked up the empty kettle and took it to the kitchen door. I knocked tentatively.

'*Komm inn!*'

My Norwegian, though I was working on it, was slight but this didn't need a translation. I went into the kitchen, letting the door swing shut behind me. The young woman I had seen topping up the egg bowl was busy now feeding her young – the skateboarders I had met on my arrival. The bigger boy recognized me at once. He said his name was Olav Aasen.

Greetings, introductions, explanations followed. Olav was sent to fetch my breakfast tray, and soon I found myself perched on a stool in front of a bare, scrubbed counter, eating ham with my egg and drinking fresh coffee. The problem of where to sit had been neatly solved.

Unfortunately it wasn't so easy to avoid those with whom I didn't wish to fraternize. Without the apology of a knock the kitchen door was suddenly flung back on its hinges and the Nazi-style East German marched in.

'There is no coffee,' he said. 'Why is there no coffee?'

Mrs Aasen leapt to her feet. 'I am sorry, Herr Horst. It's not yet ready. I will bring it as quickly as I can.'

'We are waiting. We wish it now.'

It was the way he spoke that was so offensive, rather than the words themselves. And I knew from what Olav had told me yesterday that this wasn't the first time he had made himself unpleasant to Mrs Aasen. I swung around on my stool.

'Then kindly wait outside, Herr Horst,' I said icily. 'This room is private. It is not permitted to enter here unless Frau Aasen invites you.'

Horst drew himself up and his mouth tightened with anger, but he hesitated. He couldn't place me. I had spoken German but with an English accent, he had seen me driving a Jaguar with CD plates, and my clothes, my shoes . . . His eyes flicked up and down me.

'Who are you?' he demanded.

'Jon Troy. British Embassy, Oslo.'

If Horst had been closer to me he could have read my name followed by the letters UK on my delegate's badge, so I wasn't exactly divulging secrets. He had asked a simple question. I had given a simple answer.

The result was distinctly odd. Comrade Horst became embarrassed. A dull flush stained his cheekbones and his Adam's apple went up and down as he swallowed. It made me feel like the Duke of Edinburgh or some other Royal, suddenly recognized for what he was.

Fortunately Per, the smaller boy, relieved our tension by knocking over a glass of milk and starting to cry. Mrs Aasen, with many promises to the German of coffee to come, hastened to her son's aid. I mopped some spots off the sleeve of my suit and Comrade Horst, giving me a weak smile that didn't disguise his dislike, made a reasonably dignified retreat. I could only assume he had been ordered not to become embroiled with any of the Western delegates.

'That's a bad man,' Olav said solemnly. 'You must take care, Mr Troy.'

'I'll take care,' I promised with equal solemnity, though privately I thought that Horst was far less formidable than his side-kick, Günther. 'Now I'm going to help your mother with the coffee.'

But Mrs Aasen wouldn't allow me to carry the heavy copper kettle. Which, in the circumstances, was probably lucky. I might have dropped it.

As I swung open the kitchen door for her I nearly hit Fel who was standing by the side table that held the coffee and tea things. He looked tired and there were pouches under his eyes as if he hadn't slept. Behind him was Horst's beautiful compatriot from the German Democratic Republic, Fräulein Anna Mecklen. She was wearing a white shirt and a blue linen skirt with large patch pockets. My impression was that she had just reached Fel, and I sensed rather than saw her take a folded piece of paper from her pocket and slide it along the table to him.

Fel may not have been on the top of his form but his reactions were good. His fingers closed around the paper even while he was welcoming the arrival of the coffee and wishing me a surprised good morning. The incident was over so quickly that I doubt Mrs Aasen, who was setting down the heavy kettle, noticed the transfer. It was mere chance I hadn't missed it myself.

'Good morning, Fel – Fräulein.'

I gave them what I hoped was a disinterested smile and we made some conversation. Fel was smooth. He helped himself to coffee, smiled and by a gesture intimated that he would leave me to refill the girl's cup. It was all done very easily, very casually – except that his hand was shaking so much his spoon tinkled in its saucer.

There had been that letter yesterday. It could well have been left by the East Germans. They had gone through the reception hall just ahead of me. Today, there was a surreptitious note. Was it my imagination, or had Fel expected to receive it? The whole thing was absurd. Fel, who hated all communists, would never have secret dealings with Comrade Günther and Co., and yet . . . I was filled with curiosity and some other unidentifiable and chilling emotion that might have been a premonition of fear.

* * *

41

During the rest of the morning I was too occupied to worry about my ex-father-in-law. The other UK delegates arrived and I was kept busy welcoming them, making sure they found their rooms, helping them to register for the conference and disseminating information about the host country.

There was a fair amount of confusion. A bag had been lost en route. One man had forgotten to pack his reading spectacles and needed to telephone to Edinburgh. The Minister of State hadn't bothered to mention that he was bringing along his girl-friend in the guise of a personal assistant; in order to observe the proprieties a room had to be found for her even if she didn't sleep in it.

It was lunchtime before I got them all sorted out. The day was hot. Many of the delegates were strolling in the grounds or sitting on the stone terrace, drinking beer. Among the beer drinkers I noticed Fel. Verson was with him, and a couple of men I didn't know. Fel, his shirt sleeves rolled up, appeared relaxed but he could have been putting on a show.

I collected a bottle of beer for myself and took it upstairs. After my morning's efforts I wasn't feeling particularly sociable. Besides, I was hot and sticky. I needed a wash. I took off my jacket and threw it on the bed.

It was at that moment I had what seemed to be a bright idea. I leaned out of the window. To my right was the terrace. Fel was there, and Verson. They looked as if they were settled for some while. And Fel was in his shirt sleeves as I had remembered. There was no sign of his jacket. Almost certainly it was in his room – and the note Fräulein Mecklen had passed him at breakfast could still be in the pocket.

Of course I was crazy, but I couldn't resist the temptation. I hurried down the corridor to Fel's room. I had seen the number on the official list when I was organizing the

Minister's girl-friend. There was no one around. I started to fiddle with a nail file between the door and the jamb. It was more difficult than I had expected. Before the latch retracted I was sweating.

But my luck was in. Fel's jacket was flung carelessly over the back of a chair, and crumpled in one of its pockets was the East German girl's note. I straightened it out. Written in the same black ink as had been used to address the letter that had so shocked Fel yesterday, were the words: 'Main conference hall. After 1 a.m. tonight.' There was no signature.

I was standing in the middle of the room, the note in my hand, when abruptly the door opened. I swear my heart missed a beat but, thank God, it was neither Fel nor Verson, but only a chambermaid distributing towels.

This, if I had been sensible, was when I should have fled, but I didn't. Regardless, I began to make a hurried search for the letter. The room was identical to mine and there weren't many hiding-places. I looked through the drawers and the clothes in the hanging cupboard, the desk. The briefcase was locked. The other bag was empty. I didn't find the letter.

Suddenly the sound of voices outside the door caused me to freeze. Cursing myself for getting into such a predicament, I waited. I recognized Fel's laugh. The key turned in the lock.

'Jon!'

'Hello, Fel.'

His eyes flicked from me to the briefcase, back to me, and to the photographs I was holding. I had seized them from the desk as he came in. They were a triptych, framed in alligator skin, gold cornered – the perfect gift for the rich man who wished to keep the likeness of his dear ones with him whenever he travelled. Fel's dear ones were Mary, Carol and my son, Paul.

'What the hell are you doing here?'

'Sorry, Fel. I didn't mean to intrude.'

43

'Snooping?'

'No, of course not. I've been trying to find a bed for Miss Carter, my Minister's personal assistant, who's turned up unexpectedly. The maid was bringing in your towels as I was passing here and I saw the photographs. I'm sorry. I couldn't help having a look at them.'

Fel grunted. He didn't know whether to believe me or not. The towels bore witness to my story and he could – he probably would – check with Sir Theodore. For the moment he decided to give me the benefit of the doubt. He didn't want to have a row with me.

'Okay, Jon. It's great of Paul, isn't it? I'll let you have a copy when I get home.'

'Thanks.' I replaced the triptych on the desk. I wished he had offered to send me one of Carol.

There was a tap at the door and at Fel's bidding a very short, fair man with a head too big for his body came in. 'My apologies, Maximillian. I didn't mean to interrupt,' he said in German.

'You're not interrupting, Willi. This is Jon Troy who's at the British Embassy . . .'

Fel explained. His German was fluent and his accent better than mine. It was a surprise to me. I didn't know he had any knowledge of the language. I commented.

'But naturally,' the little man said, nodding his too heavy head. 'My good friend Maximillian here is – almost a compatriot of mine.'

Fel laughed. 'I don't want to deny you, Willi, but that's rather stretching a point.' And to me. 'My mother's family came originally from Heidelberg, Jon. Didn't Carol ever mention it?'

'Yes. I think she did.'

I had forgotten. A grandmother by marriage hadn't interested me much. Nor, as regards Fel's relations with the East German trio, did it seem relevant now, no more than his

44

friendship with Herr Willi Schreiber, adviser to the Chancellor of West Germany.

I tried to be sensible. I told myself it was nothing to do with me. If Fel was having clandestine dealings with the East Germans – and clearly he was – that was his business. Fel was a VIP and, in his case, the capital letters were warranted. He was a top person – again with a capital T – an immensely powerful rich American politician, used to playing in the big league. Conceivably he was acting on behalf of a Senate Committee, even the President himself. It wasn't up to me to interfere in his affairs.

All of which was true. And, after the welcoming dinner for the delegates with its many courses and many wines I should have gone to bed, to sleep, to dream – though not of Fel and his machinations. I did get around to undressing and lying down, but I couldn't make myself comfortable.

Outside it was still daylight and the thin curtains did little to create an illusion of night. It was hot. I had to keep the windows shut. If I didn't, wasps flew in. Either way, nothing drowned the birdsong. Neither the bloody birds nor the bloody insects here seemed to have any sense of night and day. I couldn't sleep.

The trouble was I didn't believe that Fel was taking part in some high-powered operation. Conceivable it might be, but probable it wasn't. Hiding a letter under the register, sneaking a note around the breakfast cups – it was all so amateurish and unnecessary. This was an international conference on world ecology. If Fel wanted to take a stroll around the grounds with Comrades Günther and Horst, ostensibly to discuss the melting ice-cap or the threatened extinction of the whooping crane, there was nothing to prevent him. The watchful Gronski might observe the incident and store it away in the archives of his mind. Willi Schreiber might interpolate some acid comment. But it was a far safer way of communicating with the East Germans, if that were necessary, than making covert assignations.

I looked at my watch. The time was five past one. Angry with myself as much as with Fel, I got out of bed and stuck my face in a basin of cold water. The shock woke me fully. It should also have brought me to my senses, but it didn't.

I pulled on a pair of slacks and a sweater, slipped into a pair of shoes. Quietly I opened the door. The corridor outside was empty. Resisting the temptation to run, I merely hurried, my footsteps sounding loud on the wooden floor. I was beset by a sudden feeling of urgency. The note to Fel had said after 1 a.m. It was that now.

I pushed through the last of the heavy fireproof doors dividing the corridor and ran down a short flight of stairs. This brought me into an L-shaped lounging area. Here everything was in half shadow and I paused. There were sounds of voices and laughter from an adjoining sitting-room and the reflection of artificial light. Obviously some delegates were still awake.

I went across to the window from where I could see the main conference hall with its wooden bell tower. This, I knew, could be reached either by going outside and taking a path across the grass, or through a tunnel, built to protect winter delegates from the Norwegian snows, which led from a door in the angle of the L about a hundred yards underground.

The first alternative wasn't available to me. The Russian, Boris Gronski, was strolling up and down outside, taking the air and smoking the inevitable cigar. His behaviour couldn't have been more casual, more open. If it was a somewhat unlikely time for a walk, the night was warm and there was plenty of light. A man who didn't sleep too well, especially in a strange bed, might easily decide to take such a stroll. But Gronski – I didn't trust Gronski a millimetre.

Suddenly there was a heart-stopping noise behind me. I

whipped round. No one. The noise was repeated, louder. It came from the direction of a high-backed winged chair. Someone was sitting there, presumably on guard at the tunnel entrance, as Gronski might be on guard on the outdoor path.

I wondered what would happen if I walked across the room and started to open the door to the tunnel. There was only one way to find out. I walked across the room.

Admittedly I didn't expect to be shot in the back, but I did find myself counting the steps and my mouth was unpleasantly dry. I grasped the door handle. I pushed. And when absolutely nothing happened, I felt every kind of fool.

Letting the door swing shut again I turned and, as if I had just realized he was there, said: 'Did I disturb you? I'm terribly sorry.'

The reply was a repetition of the former noise – the sort of snuffling grunt that a pig makes – but this time it was easier to interpret: the man was asleep, or feigning sleep. And now he decided to wake.

After a couple of giant-sized snores he said: 'Oh, hello, Mr Troy. Sorry. I must have nodded off.' It was Herr Willi Schreiber whom I'd met in Fel's room.

'My apologies for disturbing you, sir.'

'No. No. I am grateful to you.' He glanced at his watch and mimed horror. 'Oh, *mein Gott*, I should be in bed.'

'I'll wish you good night, then, Herr Schreiber.'

'Good night to you, Mr Troy. Good night.'

The little man made no excuse to hang around. Shaking his heavy head as if in self-reproach for being up so late, he trotted away. I waited a full minute.

There was a burst of raucous laughter from the adjoining sitting-room, the conclusion of a blue story perhaps, other sounds. The party could be breaking up and I didn't want to be embroiled with some half-drunk delegates. I had already

47

wasted too much time. Hurriedly I opened the tunnel door and slipped through.

The darkness was total. I paused. Jane, in spite of all her forethought, hadn't suggested I equip myself with a torch, and I had to let my eyes adjust. In my mind I visualized the tunnel which I had been along earlier that day when I was exploring the centre.

As I remembered it, a flight of steep steps led down to the passage which ran straight to the conference hall. However, because of the slope of the ground, only three or four steps were needed at the far end to bring one to the right level. Once there, if I could push open the door an inch or two I should be able to see – by the light coming through the windows – whom Fel was meeting, perhaps even hear something of what was being said.

I groped for the wall beside me. My fingers touched the electric light switch, which I didn't dare to use, and brushed against some curtains. It was then I recalled the alcoves set in the tunnel walls at regular intervals. These contained stacks of chairs, books, oddments, and were all neatly curtained. They would be excellent hiding-places for me if Fel or one of the East Germans emerged from the conference hall unexpectedly.

They would be excellent hiding-places for anyone. And I wondered what the hell I was doing here, what I hoped to achieve.

Swallowing my unease, I began to edge down the steps and I must have been within reach of the bottom when there was a heavy muffled thud from further along the passage. This was followed by a half-suppressed oath in what I took to be English, and by sounds of scuffling.

I stopped dead, held my breath and listened. Interpreting the noises, I decided that two men, hampered by the darkness, were struggling with each other. They were trying to be as quiet as they could, but the tunnel magnified the noise they couldn't help making. I heard thumps, grunts, harsh panting. One of them seemed to be getting the worst of it. I hoped it wasn't Fel.

Before I could decide whether or not to interfere, there was a sharp click and the length of the tunnel was illuminated. I got a very clear picture of the two men. Neither of them was Fel. I was sure of that, though I caught only a glimpse of the character lying on the ground, not enough to recognize him. Afterwards I thought he might have been Comrade Horst.

I was in no doubt about his opponent. It was Robert F. Verson. Startled by the sudden light, his arms dropped to his sides and he stared straight at me. The tableau lasted no more than a couple of seconds. The other man recovered first. His knee came up and crashed into Verson's groin.

That was the last thing I saw. It was my own fault. I was looking directly at the struggling men and beyond them at the steps leading up to the door to the conference hall. There was no one standing there, no one who could have switched on the light at that end of the tunnel. Which meant there was someone behind me. But I didn't work this out until too late.

Something hit me, hard and expertly, behind the ear, and I blacked out.

Chapter Three

IT WAS MY recurrent nightmare come to life again. Once more I was lying on the ground. People were clustered around me. I felt bruised, sick, giddy. Shapes slanted towards me, hung poised to collapse and at the critical moment, when I knew I was about to be crushed, fell back. I breathed hard.

My eyes were tight shut. I didn't dare open them. I knew what I would see if I did, police, ambulance, Fel's smashed-up Cadillac, the hateful face of Darlene Smith's husband as he prepared to kick me in the ribs, to spit on me, to . . . I cried out.

'No! No! It was an accident. I wasn't drunk. It's not true. I never – '

'My dear chap, no one's suggesting you were drunk.'

'You slipped on the steps, Herr Troy, and hit your head.'

'Sure. It was an accident. Those steps are real dangerous.'

They spoke with a confusion of voices and a variety of accents, but they were all friendly. One of them had his arm around me and was pillowing the upper part of my body against him. Another carefully laid his jacket over me. There was no feeling of animosity. I opened my eyes.

'Good, he's coming round.'

'Maybe we should get a doctor. He could be concussed.'

'Let's move him first. It's goddam cold in this tunnel.'

I looked up at them, at their kind, worried faces. I recognized the ornithologist, Simpson-Brown, a couple of

Americans I had seen with Fel, Herr Willi Schreiber – and Herr Comrade Werner Günther. It was Günther who was supporting me.

I recognized the tunnel and I knew where I was. I could have wept with relief. I didn't care that it was probably one of these men who had slugged me – most likely Schreiber or Günther. The nightmare was only a nightmare and it was over. I was in Norway, not in the States, and no one was about to accuse me of rape or anything else.

'I'm – I'm okay,' I said. 'At least I think I am.'

I struggled to sit up and eventually, with some help and general encouragement, managed to stand. Leaning on the taller American I made it slowly and laboriously up the steps and into the lounge. The world threatened to spin about me, but with an effort of will I was able to steady it. I have felt worse.

My rescuers gathered round, making various suggestions. A doctor should be found to examine me. I should be given brandy. I should not be given brandy. I should be put to bed. The last appealed to me most, though I was recovering fast and by now was capable of putting myself to bed.

'Thank you all very much,' I said. 'I'm sorry to have been a nuisance. Perhaps if one of you would help me – ' I looked hopefully at Simpson-Brown, who responded immediately.

'Of course, my dear chap.' He took me by the arm. 'Come along.'

'We will say good night then.' Willie Schreiber nodded his big head at me. 'We are pleased you are okay. You might have been badly hurt, Mr Troy. It was dangerous to go down there in the dark.'

While I debated whether the West German intended to give me a warning, the East German said, 'Yes, indeed, Herr Troy. It is not advisable to be so – so enterprising.' And the smaller of the Americans added: 'Sure isn't, Mr Troy, not if you're going to get yourself concussed.'

51

Everyone laughed and in return I managed a weak smile. But it was an effort. I didn't like being threatened.

'Bed!' Simpson-Brown said firmly.

There was a chorus of good nights and I repeated my thanks. Half-reluctant, I let the ornithologist lead me away. Thoughts were slipping in and out of my mind. I glanced surreptitiously at my watch. I couldn't be accurate about the time but, as best I could judge, my black-out in the tunnel hadn't lasted more than five minutes.

In those five minutes a lot must have happened.

First, both Verson and the man he was struggling with had succeeded in disappearing. Logic indicated that one of them – God knew which – had got out of the tunnel before the influx of my rescuers and that the other had hidden or been hidden behind the convenient curtains of an alcove.

Secondly there was Fel and whoever he had been secretly meeting. They would have tried to get away from the conference hall without being seen. With disturbances in the tunnel and Boris Gronski strolling round the grounds outside, I decided they were unlikely to have made it.

Lastly, there was the guy who had bludgeoned me. He too must have taken some action during that brief time.

'Here we are,' Simpson-Brown said. 'Do you have your key?'

I gave it to him. I was regretting the questions I hadn't asked, questions which might sound odd in the morning. But it was too late now, except for Simpson-Brown.

'Was it you who found me, sir?'

'No. The German, Herr Schreiber, found you. He was looking for a book he'd mislaid when he heard some funny noises in the tunnel and went to investigate.'

'And – ' I prompted.

'And? Oh – you mean, what did he do? He came dashing into the sitting-room where we were having a sort of party. You know, no one can sleep in the summer in Norway unless

52

they're used to it, so it's simpler not to try. Much better get together and . . .'

Simpson-Brown was a verbose man – perhaps it was a reaction from many hours spent in solitary hides – and it was difficult to interrupt him. I concentrated on undressing and getting myself into bed. Suddenly I was aware he had repeated a question.

'Sorry, sir. What did you say?'

'I said you never told us what you were doing in the tunnel.'

'Oh, like everyone else I couldn't sleep and I decided to collect some papers I'd left in the conference hall. I'd have done better to have joined your drinking party, wouldn't I?'

'Yes. The Yanks were good fun.'

'And Herr Günther.'

'Ah, he arrived somewhat late, shortly before Herr Schreiber came to tell us of your – er – accident. Nice man, Willi Schreiber, don't you think? He was genuinely, most genuinely, upset about you.'

I regarded Simpson-Brown speculatively. He was standing in the middle of the room on his left leg, the right leg tucked up, not unlike one of his cranes. It was a favourite position of his and one which, since he was tall and thin with wispy grey hair, made him appear somewhat absurd. But it was the only absurd thing about him. His eyes were bright with humour and intelligence.

'If I had to bet, I'd bet on Herr Günther,' he said, excluding persons unknown of course. From what I've observed of him I would say his behaviour was out of character – definitely out of character. He's not the Good Samaritan type at all. And that makes him suspect, doesn't it?'

He grinned at me and I hesitated. Though Simpson-Brown inspired confidence I couldn't explain, not without involving Fel. Yet I couldn't seem too much of a cretin either. The bird-man was very observant.

53

'Are you – are you suggesting that I didn't slip on those stairs?' I asked slowly. 'That someone – '

'My dear chap, you've a lump, duck-egg size, under your ear. You didn't get that by banging your head on any step. You were slugged.'

'Well – thanks for telling me.'

'As if you didn't know.' He laughed. 'No matter. I can mind my own business. Are you all right now, Jon? If so I'll be getting along.'

'I'm fine, thank you, sir. Good night.'

He nodded affably. 'Have a good sleep and stay in bed in the morning. I'll organize breakfast for you.'

The door shut behind Simpson-Brown and I put up a tentative hand. I felt the back of my neck. As the birdman had said, it was one hell of a lump. I could scarcely bear to touch it. And I thought long and earnestly of Herr Werner Günther of the Deutsche Demokratische Republik and of my former father-in-law, Maximillian Felard. I was still thinking of them as I drifted into sleep. My thoughts were not charitable.

My first visitor arrived shortly before eight a.m. Simpson-Brown wanted to know the state of my health, what I would like for breakfast. Next came Herr Schreiber, who was equally solicitous. He was closely followed by Mrs Aasen, bearing my breakfast tray.

I was beginning to enjoy my role of invalid when my fourth visitor appeared. It was Fel, and he was in a foul temper. He didn't bother with the niceties. He didn't care a bloody damn how I was feeling. He had come to tell me where I got off and he was going to do just that.

'Jon, I don't know what the hell you think you're up to, but it's going to stop – as of this moment. Do you understand? I will not have you snooping in my room – searching through my clothes, I don't doubt – and following me around, spying on me. I will not have it, Jon!'

54

He had clenched his big fist and, finding nowhere convenient to thump it down, shook it at me. I didn't remember seeing him so fraught ever before. I had seen him angry, but his anger had always been controlled, based on the knowledge that in the long run he would triumph. Now he seemed to have lost his usual overweening self-confidence. And he was mean.

'You, Jon, with your goddam interference, poking your nose into my affairs, you've ruined a meeting that was very carefully set up, a meeting of the utmost importance to me.'

'A meeting with Werner Günther?'

The words slipped out. Immediately I wished them unsaid. The colour drained from Fel's face leaving it a peculiar mottled shade under the tan. He leaned over me, menacing. He was breathing heavily and his breath smelt sour. For a split second I thought he was going to strike me. Then he straightened himself. It seemed to require a physical effort.

He said thickly, as if his tongue was too big for his mouth: 'Keep out of my way, Jon! If you don't, I'll break you into little pieces, and don't think because you're a goddam Limey I can't. If you cause me any more trouble I'll ruin you, boy. I'll really screw you. Do you hear?'

He didn't give me a chance to answer. He slammed from the room, leaving me shaken – and resentful. I knew that his threats weren't empty, that he wouldn't hesitate to implement them, but – I told myself there were no 'buts'. After this I would be every kind of fool to thwart him.

I poured myself some more coffee and considered getting up. The idea was not particularly appealing. I hadn't felt too bad until Fel's explosive visit. Now my head had started to throb, gently but steadily.

I was busy cursing my ex-father-in-law when there was another knock at the door. My room had become like Charing Cross Station in the rush hour. I said: 'Come in,' but with no enthusiasm.

In came Robert F. Verson. Of all the people at the Lysebu conference centre Verson was the least expected and the least welcome; but that wasn't what made me gawp at him.

Verson – the suave, correct Ivy Leaguer – looked like some badly crippled ex-boxer. One side of his face was bruised and swollen, and he must have lost a couple of teeth because his voice came out in a sort of muffled whisper. But what was most noticeable was the way he walked, as if it hurt like hell. I rather hoped it did.

'I want to talk with you,' he said, 'about last night. You were in the tunnel. I saw you when that guy switched the lights on.'

'What guy?'

'Christ knows. I didn't recognize him. The lights were on only for a second and he was holding the drapes in front of him. What happened next? I suppose he slugged you.' He didn't wait for me to confirm it. 'That's when I got the chop myself. And just let me get my hands on the bastard who did it to me.'

'You recognized him, then?'

'I did not, dammit. He took me from behind in the dark. You know who he was?'

I shook my head and wished I hadn't. Verson was being very frank, too frank. I couldn't work out what he wanted.

'Well, I doubt he'll claim the credit for what he did to me.' Verson gave a lop-sided smile. 'So that leaves you, Jon, and lucky for me it's you, isn't it?'

'I don't understand.' It was true, but I tried to make it sound like a lie. Confusion to the enemy was always a good gambit. 'You'll have to spell it out.'

'Okay. It's really very simple. I lied to Fel. I told him I went for a walk last night, up in the woods, and I was mugged. I had to account for my appearance someways.' Verson tenderly touched the side of his face. In spite of himself he winced. 'And you, Jon, are going to support that story if the need arises. You never saw me in the tunnel last night. Is that clear?'

'Perfectly clear, yes.' I sneered at him. 'You've been spying on Fel and you're scared I'll tell him. That's quite a turn-up.'

Verson gave me a long, cold stare. 'I'm not asking any favours from you, Jon. It's not necessary. Remember Darlene Smith. Of course no one wants to rake up that old business again, but a word or two sewn in Washington diplomatic circles would soon grow into a fine, strong rumour, and there's nothing so difficult to quash as a rumour. I've known a mere hint of scandal ruin a man's career, and in your case rape, well . . .'

You sod, I thought, you perfect sod. Aloud I said, 'Okay, Verson. Okay. I understand. If it's that important to you. You were nowhere near the tunnel last night. Now, get out!'

'As long as you don't forget – '

'I won't.'

I shut my eyes and kept them shut until the door closed behind him. Then I staggered out of bed. My stomach was churning. I made it to the toilet and was noisily, satisfactorily sick. Afterwards I shoved my head under the shower and let the water come down, hard and fast and cold. It made me feel a little better, but not much.

In the afternoon I drove down to Fornebu to fetch a bag lost by one of the British delegates. The airport authorities had telephoned to say that it had turned up on another flight from Copenhagen.

The bag was a good excuse to get away from the conference centre and, having collected it, I decided to play truant. Everyone was busy at various meetings, bewailing the mess we all had made, were making and were likely to make of the world's environment. No one was going to miss me. I headed for the Embassy.

Almost the first person I met in the corridor was Jane

Hamlin, staggering under a pile of files. In spite of her burden she looked cool and attractive in a green linen dress that suited her. The sudden joy that flooded her face at the sight of me almost made me wish I was in love with her. It would have been so pleasant and so uncomplicated.

'Here, let me help you with those.'

'Thanks, Jon.' She gave me a wide smile as I took the files from her. 'You're just the man I wanted to see. I was going to phone you.'

'What about? Not my leave?' I was suddenly anxious.

'Yes. It's due to start next Monday, isn't it?'

'Oh, Christ! Don't tell me. Duncan's mum requested her ashes be scattered in a dozen different places so he won't be back and my leave's cancelled.'

'No. It's not that. We're expecting Duncan on Thursday at latest.' Jane held the door of her office open for me and I dumped the files on her desk. 'Thanks, Jon. Would you like some tea?'

'Please. I'd love some, but – is H.E. in?'

'No. He's gone to NATO headquarters for the day.'

'To Kolsas? Did he say why?' She shook her head and I shrugged. 'Oh well, at least he won't want to know what I'm doing here when I'm meant to be out at Lysebu.'

Half my mind anxious about my leave, the other half worrying at what H.E. might be up to – after all, defence was my business and if it hadn't been for Duncan's mum I would almost certainly have been out at Kolsas with him – I watched Jane make tea. Duncan's mum, I thought wryly, had a lot to answer for as far as I was concerned. If it hadn't been for her, I would never have been near the World Environment Conference or got myself involved again with Fel, or with Verson or the East Germans . . .

'Jon!'

'Sorry. What were you saying?'

'This cousin of mine – she's a medical student – is coming

58

to visit me for a week, and I was wondering, since you won't be here – '

'You want to borrow my flat?'

'I'd be terribly grateful, Jon. Otherwise it means the sofa in my living-room, and that becomes a bit sordid after a couple of days. She's not the most tidy of girls.'

'Does she break things?'

'No. I don't think so.' Jane laughed. 'Anyway, she wouldn't go into your flat. I'd just use it for sleeping – if that's all right with you.'

'Of course it is. I'll give you a door key today. I've a spare in my office safe. When's your cousin arriving?'

'The noon flight on Monday.'

'That's fine. I'm catching the Saturday night ferry to Frederikshavn. The place is yours as long as I'm away. May I suggest the balcony for breakfast. There's a marvellous view of Oslofjord.'

'Thank you, Jon. It's very kind of you.' Suddenly she flushed. 'Jon, it really is a girl cousin.'

'Dearest Jane, I don't doubt it. Otherwise you wouldn't need an extra bed, would you?'

By the time I left the Embassy I felt altogether happier. Jane always seemed to have the ability to cheer me up and I was looking forward to my leave – a long, solitary drive through Northern Europe and ten blissful days in my house in Brittany. The thought filled me with a deep pleasure. I could scarcely wait till Saturday.

Chapter Four

THE NEXT DAY was Midsummer's Eve. It began peacefully. The morning was devoted to sectional meetings and, to show willing, I went along to the bird people's gathering which was being chaired by Simpson-Brown. It was a comparatively small group and I soon realized that the discussion was likely to be far too technical for me. However, I had nothing better to do and I was out of the way of Fel and Verson and the East Germans, which was a big advantage.

I chose a seat near the door, prayed there would be a lot of slides and gave myself up to quiet contemplation. Among the mail I had picked up at the Embassy yesterday had been a letter from the Breton farmer who keeps an eye on my house. He said everything was ready for me but the living-room floor, which had been sagging for some time, was getting worse. He had taken up the carpet and in his opinion a large section of the flooring needed replacement. You could see right through to the cellar below.

I blew out a sigh. My bank balance was still in the red after buying the Jaguar and the threatened expense of a new floor was ill-timed. I didn't envy the Felards their money, but there were times . . .

Simpson-Brown was launched on a set of statistics and I was wondering if I would have to spend my leave wood-working when the door was tentatively opened. Immediately my thoughts were jolted to the here and now. And Simpson-Brown lost nine-tenths of his audience's attention.

Caught in a shaft of sun, her pale red hair shining, Anna Mecklen stood poised on the threshold. She couldn't have looked more beautiful. The world's bird population didn't stand a chance against her.

'Come in, Dr Mecklen. Come in. We've been expecting you to join us.'

Simpson-Brown may have been expecting her but I certainly wasn't. I wasn't aware she knew a hedgesparrow from a housesparrow. I had assumed – I admit without giving the matter any thought – that she was some sort of PA to Comrades Günther and Horst and the idea of a doctorate threw me.

'I apologize, Professor. I didn't intend to be late but I had difficulty finding the right room.'

'No matter, my dear.' Simpson-Brown beamed on her; it was obvious the old boy was as taken with her as anyone else. 'We're delighted you've arrived. You must know how we value your expertise.'

'Thank you.'

She bowed her head and smiled. Her smile, primarily directed at Simpson-Brown, somehow included me. She sat down beside me, put on a pair of enormous spectacles and produced a pad and pencil. She listened with the greatest attention; made the occasional note. But when the discussion became general any suspicion I might have had that she was a phoney was dissipated. Whatever else she might be Dr Anna Mecklen was a *bona fide* bird-woman. Simpson-Brown hadn't been flattering her when he spoke of her expertise.

During the coffee break I tried to enlarge the conversation. The bird people were all keen types. They were only interested in their own beloved subject, and my contribution – that the flamingoes at Buckingham Palace had recently been decimated by some unknown virus – was not a success. It met with a polite blankness as befitted a non-scholarly, non-relevant remark.

61

I thought of leaving but before I had taken any action Simpson-Brown called the meeting to order and Anna indicated that we should again sit down. I could scarcely refuse such an invitation.

And later when the meeting was over she deliberately chose to walk with me across the grass to the main building. It seemed she had suddenly become interested in me. She enquired about my accident in the tunnel and she wanted to know what I, a non-environmentalist, was doing at Lysebu. She was very convincing, but not convincing enough if – which I very much doubted – her object was to please me. Nevertheless, I was happy to answer her questions and regretted their interruption by the Minister of State's girl-friend.

'Jon, Sir Theodore wants to know what arrangements you've made for tonight. Have you laid on an embassy car for us?'

'No, I haven't.'

'Why not? You can't expect us to walk three-quarters of a mile and then take that silly tram down to Holmenkollen. It's a formal dinner. I shall be wearing a long dress.'

I swallowed the retort I would have liked to make. At least the little bitch had confirmed my dogsbody role at the conference. And for a moment I felt the pressure of Anna's hand on my arm.

'Goodbye for now, Mr Troy.'

'*Auf Wiedersehen, Fräulein.*' I turned to the other girl. 'I'll make enquiries and let you know. I'm sure the Norwegians are laying on some transport.'

'But what about an embassy car for Sir Theodore?' She was petulant. 'The Americans provide one for that Mr Felard all the time.'

'Miss Carter, my ex-father-in-law happens to be an important man,' I said acidly.

And grinning at her amazement I walked away and left

her. It didn't seem to matter that I might have made an enemy.

I had been wrong about the transport. The Norwegians who were to be our hosts for the Midsummer's Eve celebration had made no arrangements, and the result was confusion confounded. Very few of the delegates had cars. Taxis could be ordered, but the charge was estimated from Oslo and that made them an expensive proposition. The alternative was to go by the tram that cut through the mountainside more or less parallel to the road. Unfortunately it was a long walk to the nearest tram stop.

In the event, however, there wasn't much choice. The majority had to go on foot and by tram. The UK delegates were among the lucky ones. I ordered a taxi for the Minister and his trollop and, thanks to Simpson-Brown who sat the lady soil-erosion expert on his lap, managed to stuff the rest of the Brits into my Jag.

When we arrived at the restaurant I dropped them off at the entrance and drove around to the carpark by myself. As I manœuvred into place the East Germans' Volvo drew in beside me. To my surprise Werner Günther was driving. He too was alone.

'Herr Troy, how are you? You have recovered, I hope, from your unpleasant experience last night?' The smile didn't reach his eyes.

'Thank you, yes,' I said, taking care to keep my voice non-committal. 'It was a stupid accident, wasn't it? I should have been more careful.'

He made some casual comment and, since I didn't want to be downright uncivil, I found myself walking across the carpark with him. While I listened, he talked – about the extinction of animals as a result of man's usurping their territories. I must admit he sounded quite knowledgeable, and I was in no position to expose any errors he might have made. All the same I would have bet that the information he was so happily imparting to me was available in popular paperbacks. Even after Dr Mecklen I couldn't bring myself to believe in Comrade Günther as an environmentalist.

'Troy! Come here!'

The peremptory summons came from the Minister of State as Günther and I reached the restaurant and, though I was glad of an excuse to be rid of the East German, I obeyed reluctantly. Sir Theodore, a short, pompous, middle-aged man, who smelled too loudly of after-shave, was standing by the taxi that had brought him down from the conference centre. His bulbous eyes were shining with annoyance; he was angry and someone was going to be sorry for it.

Clearly it wasn't going to be the taxi-driver, who sat stolidly behind the wheel waiting to receive what he knew was due to him. Nor was it going to be Miss Carter in her tight-fitting, sexy dress. That left an unfortunate Norwegian who had been trying to sort out the difficulty, and me.

'This driver's a rogue,' Sir Theodore said loudly. 'He's asking a ludicrous fare and pretends he doesn't understand my English. See to it, Troy, will you?'

He marched off before I could answer, followed by the girl who gave me a triumphant glance of pure malice. There were a lot of people around and she was pleased to see me humiliated – as she thought – in front of them.

I paid the taxi-driver – adding a large tip as recompense for Sir Theodore's unpleasantness even though it was unlikely I would be able to reclaim it – did my best to placate the Norwegian, and went up the steps to the restaurant. By the door I saw Boris Gronski, who must have had a splendid view of my arrival. Tactfully he pretended not to see me.

The dinner was a superb feast. From the salmon trout through the reindeer to the lemon sorbet – luckily cloud-berries were out of season – the food was delicious and the wines carefully chosen. The Norwegians had done us proud.

They had also had the sense to keep speeches to the minimum. There was a welcoming speech from the Norwegian Secretary of the Environment at the beginning of the meal and a thank-you speech on behalf of the delegates with the dessert. That was all. For a Scandinavian occasion it was surprisingly informal and, to quote Simpson-Brown, 'very jolly'.

As the wine took hold everyone relaxed. The number of private *skols* increased and I found myself, my fingers caressing the stem of my glass, trying to catch Fräulein Mecklen's eye. I wasn't the only one. To my amusement I saw several of the ornithologists who had met Anna without the forbidding presence of Günther or Horst lift their glasses towards her. But they drank alone. She ignored the lot of us.

It was during the cheese, after they had lost interest and when both the East German comrades were preoccupied, that I chanced to see Anna raise her glass in the direction of the high table, sip the wine and replace the glass. Her gesture was definite but quick, and I was slow to pinpoint her partner in the *skol*. But it might have been Fel. I was almost sure it was, though I could have been wrong.

While I was considering this, the Norwegian Secretary rose, followed by the rest of the high table. The dinner was over. There would be an interval so that the tables could be cleared and rearranged, and a general post take place before coffee was served. Most of the delegates seized the chance to go outside on to the terrace. Many of them went to the cloakroom first. There was much to-ing and fro-ing.

I wandered round, had a chat with a Frenchman who came from Brittany, decided that by this time the Gents' would be moderately empty and made for it. Someone called to me.

'Mr Troy, come. Come, please.'

A Norwegian woman whom I recognized as being in charge of conference arrangements was waving agitatedly at me. She was obviously upset. I couldn't ignore her wild semaphoring, but it wasn't until I reached her that I realized she was blocking Fräulein Anna Mecklen from my view.

Anna was leaning against the wall. She was pale perhaps, but otherwise she didn't look ill. Yet she seemed to be in some distress. Her eyes were shut and one hand pressed her forehead as she frowned fiercely. It was a theatrical pose that made me regard her doubtfully.

The Norwegian had no doubts. She said anxiously, 'The Fräulein is unwell. She nearly fainted in the ladies' cloakroom and her head hurts. She would like her friends to take her back to the conference centre so that she may go to bed.'

'I'm sure that can be arranged,' I said.

'Please forgive me, Mr Troy.' Anna opened her eyes and gave me a weak smile. 'I don't wish to be a trouble, but this lady doesn't know my colleagues Herr Günther and Herr Horst. You would recognize them, I think?'

I hesitated. I could easily run the beautiful German girl back to Lysebu myself. The idea was tempting though, in view of Fel's attitude to me and the East Germans, perhaps not particularly wise.

'If you could find her friends, I will stay with her until you return, Mr Troy.'

'Yes, of course, I'll go – '

I wasn't allowed to complete the sentence. Fel loomed beside me. He appeared to size up the situation immediately, and to take control.

'This is no place for you if you're feeling ill, Fräulein,' he said in German. 'My car's outside. Permit me to drive you back to the centre – I have a slight headache myself and would be happy to leave the dinner.'

'Thank you. Thank you very much. You are most kind.'

'And your colleagues, Fräulein?' the Norwegian asked.

Anna looked at me. 'Perhaps Mr Troy would be good enough to tell them?'

Fel didn't give me a chance to agree of my own accord. 'Yes. You do that, Jon,' he ordered, taking Anna by the arm and starting to lead her away. 'You'll find them somewhere around, I'm sure.'

Dismissed like a small boy who had been making a nuisance of himself, I nodded to the Norwegian woman and departed in search of Günther and Horst. I didn't hurry. Fel hadn't given the impression that there was any urgency. In fact, though I was prepared to take him at his word, I was far from certain that he wanted the East Germans in hot pursuit.

I set off in the direction of the stairs. People were beginning to return to the dining-room in expectation of coffee. Thinking that the comrades were probably among them, I joined the throng, and found myself in the company of Boris Gronski.

'Ah, Mr Troy. I trust you enjoyed the dinner our Norwegian hosts were so kind to offer us. A veritable banquet, wasn't it?'

'Yes. Magnificent.'

'It's amazing what a difference to a country the finding of oil can make. I remember visiting Norway in nineteen-seventy and – '

Gronski stopped speaking. I was never to know his opinion of the Norwegian economy during the last decade. Someone was racing downstairs with giant strides, scattering apologies that sounded more like imprecations as he bored through the ascending stream of delegates. Robert F. Verson was in a hell of a hurry, and regardless of the disturbance he was causing.

As Verson drew level with us, Gronski deliberately thrust out his foot. Verson didn't have a chance. With a wild shriek he proceeded to give an excellent imitation of a diver who had changed his mind too late and been forced by the law of gravity to take off in spite of himself. His belly flop was spectacular.

Beside me I felt Gronski wince in sympathy. Then he was urging me to the rescue. Together we helped Verson to stand. He was winded, but as far as one could judge from his already battered appearance otherwise unhurt. The fall, however, had not improved his temper. He swore savagely.

'My dear Mr – er – Verson,' Gronski said, reading the name-card on Verson's lapel. 'Are you all right? I'm so very sorry. It was an accident, I assure you. I slipped and my foot kicked out involuntarily. I do apologize. I wouldn't have had it happen for the world.'

Gronski's fulsomeness gave Verson time to control himself. 'That's okay, Mr – er – Gronski,' he hissed through the gap in his teeth. 'Forget it.'

'I should have been more careful, but I was talking to my friend here – Jon Troy. Do you know Mr Troy?' Gronski continued to be voluble. 'He'll tell you how – '

'Yeah! I know Troy. And, if you'll excuse me – '

But Gronski had no desire to excuse him. He dusted imaginary dust from Verson's suit. He produced his cigar case.

'Allow me to offer you one of these. A small recompense, Mr Verson. They're the best Havana. I have them imported from Cuba, a privilege at present denied to you Americans, alas.'

'I don't smoke,' Verson all but thrust Gronski out of his way. 'If you'll excuse me,' he said again. 'There's something I have to do.'

Gronski watched him go. 'Poor man,' he said sadly. 'Last night he was mugged in the woods, I'm told, and tonight he has this unfortunate experience.'

Po-faced, I agreed. 'Most unfortunate.'

'Of course, he did ask for it – dashing down the stairs like that. You wouldn't know what was so urgent for him, I suppose, Mr Troy?'

'No idea.'

I lied. I could have made a very good guess. Verson had seen Fel leaving the restaurant with Fräulein Mecklen and, reasonably enough, was curious to know what was going on – just as I was. But it was not my business. Once again I told myself that, and murmuring a goodbye to Gronski I renewed my search for Comrades Günther and Horst.

I found them upstairs in the dining-room, which by now had been rearranged for coffee. Most of the delegates were seated in groups, but the comrades were standing in the doorway talking earnestly to each other. I made the message simple – Fräulein Mecklen wished them to know that she had a bad headache and Mr Felard had kindly offered to drive her back to the conference centre. There was no cause to worry about her.

They weren't worried. They were positively alarmed. Horst especially became very agitated, and in the stress of the moment forgot that at our meeting in Mrs Aasen's kitchen I had spoken fluent, if not accentless, German.

'We must follow them immediately, immediately,' he said to Günther. 'We don't know what she might not – '

'Be quiet, you fool!' Günther ordered grimly. Then, turning to me with a smile, he spoke in English, 'We're disturbed by what you've told us, Herr Troy. Fräulein Mecklen hasn't been at all well lately. We must go after her at once and make sure everything is being done for her that should be done. You understand?'

I didn't understand but I said I did and they hurried away. Five or so minutes later, while I was having coffee with Simpson-Brown and Herr Schreiber, who seemed to have struck up an unexpected friendship with each other, Günther reappeared. He made straight for me.

'Herr Troy, forgive me. I don't want to disturb you but we need your help. We want to return to the conference centre, as you know, and our car won't start. Horst has done every-thing he can, but it's useless. Would you be kind enough to drive us?'

'Well – ' I said hesitantly.

My reluctance was obvious, and Simpson-Brown said coldly, 'The space in Mr Troy's car is already promised, Herr Günther. I'm afraid you'll have to walk or patronize the tram.'

Günther regarded him with a fish-eye. 'You don't under-stand. Fräulein Mecklen has been taken ill. It's imperative we go now.'

'Ah, that's different. Of course Jon must . . .'

'In that case I'm sure Herr Troy . . .'

To my annoyance Simpson-Brown and Schreiber, mis-interpreting what Günther had said – as he had probably intended – spoke in unison and committed me.

'All right!' I was damned if I was going to start explaining about Fel. 'Since you're so anxious about Fräulein Mecklen, Herr Günther, I'll run you up to the centre and come back later to collect Mr Simpson-Brown and the others.'

Gratitude wasn't natural to Comrade Günther, but he did his best. 'Thank you, Herr Troy. It's very good of you. Thank you.'

Full of suppressed irritation, I nodded an uncharitable goodbye to Simpson-Brown and Schreiber and let Günther usher me out of the dining-room. We went in silence down the stairs and out of the restaurant, neither the comrade nor I volunteering any remark. I assumed that both of us were having black thoughts about Fel and Anna, but the irony of this failed to activate my sense of humour. I was feeling more bloody-minded by the minute.

Nevertheless, as Günther set off at a smart pace across the carpark, I followed. Fel was long gone. There was no sign of Verson. But next to my Jaguar stood Horst, poking around disconsolately in the Volvo's engine.

70

Günther, trying to sound affable but at the same time determined to get going, said, 'Come along. Let's be quick. Mr Troy's giving us a lift, but he has to return here afterwards.'

I unlocked the Jag but didn't move away from the door. Instead I stared meaningly at Horst's hands which were filthy from the attempted car repairs. I didn't want grease all over the Jag's upholstery. Günther's response was immediate. He made an angry gesture that couldn't have been more explicit. Horst obeyed. He took out his handkerchief and wiped his hands. But as I stood aside to let him into the back seat the look he gave me was venomous.

I didn't care. I started the Jag and drove out of the carpark. Glancing at my watch I saw it was almost midnight, which meant it was as dark as it was going to be, that is to say on the edge of dusk, and when we turned on to the winding mountain road where there were overhanging trees and patches of shadow I switched on the headlights.

Minutes later, as we swung around a bend, they illuminated a solitary figure walking grimly uphill. Giving Verson ten out of ten for determination, I hooted, stopped a few yards ahead of him, and waited. After Comrades Günther and Horst the Jaguar was going to need fumigating anyway, and adding Verson to the passenger list wouldn't make much difference. Besides, it was worth offering Verson a lift to watch the expression on his face as he recognized the East Germans.

He didn't thank me. Indeed, I think that for a split second he was tempted to refuse to come with us, but it was a long haul to the conference centre. Sullenly he got into the back next to Horst. And once more we set off.

I drove fast – I was eager to be rid of my unwanted cargo – and we must have got two-thirds of the way to Lysebu when the Jag coughed. It coughed again, a racking cancer-of-the-lungs cough, and the motor died. I couldn't believe it. I had just had the car serviced because of my proposed trip to Brittany and it was running splendidly.

I did the obvious things, tried to restart the engine, checked the petrol, made sure no vital wire had come loose. Then I gave up. From the cough it was probably carburettor trouble, but I'm no mechanic. The garage would have to cope in the morning.

I said, 'Gentlemen, I'm sorry but it seems to be a night for break-downs. This is as far as we go.'

To my surprise the comrades took it very well. Horst offered reasonable advice and, when that failed, did yeoman service pushing the Jag off the road into a clearing in the woods where regretfully I locked and left it. Günther co-operated and even expressed sympathy. Only Verson was vituperative, as if I were to blame. Once assured that the Jag couldn't be restarted, he stormed ahead of us up the hill.

It was a mistake on his part. The second car to overtake us stopped. It had room for two. Günther as an older man was the inevitable first choice but Verson, had he been with us, might have ousted Horst. I was never in contention.

Fretting about the Jag and what would happen if the garage couldn't get it going again for my leave on Saturday, I plodded on. This was a hell of a way to spend Midsummer's Eve. To cheer myself I thought of last year when Jane and I had been invited on to a yacht, from which we had skolled in champagne the bonfires being lit around the fjord. That had been a party worth remembering. But this year . . .

I was thankful to reach the end of the drive leading to the centre. From the lodge where the Aasens lived and which was in darkness, I cut across the grass. No one was about. By now Fräulein Mecklen was probably asleep, Comrades Günther and Horst undressing and Verson brushing his teeth. I lengthened my stride. I would have to telephone the restaurant and warn Simpson-Brown I wouldn't be returning.

After that I was for bed and forgetting the whole bloody evening.

But the evening wasn't over yet. As I came round the corner of the conference hall I stopped in my tracks. A man was climbing out of one of the upper windows in the main building. For several seconds he hung by his arms, then let himself go. He landed awkwardly but it wasn't a long drop and on to grass. I waited for him to pick himself up.

He didn't move. He lay there in a big, heavy heap. And I began to run, fast.

Chapter Five

IN THE HALF-LIGHT he was grey and his breathing was laboured. He tried to stand but only succeeded in getting on to his hands and knees. He looked up at me, his eyes full of hate.

'Damn you, Jon! Help me!'

'Of course. But wait for a minute or two, Fel, and you'll feel better.' I hoped I was right. I didn't know what was the matter with him, if he were seriously injured or had just winded himself.

'No. Now. I must get away from here.' He began to crawl.

'For Christ's sake, Fel!' I protested.

'Keep your goddam voice low,' he said hoarsely, savagely. Even in his present state he was authoritative. 'And help me up, Jon.'

Fel was a big, heavy man and it needed all my strength to lift him under the arms and prop him against the wall. From that position he was able to shift his weight to my shoulders and with support to walk, slowly and laboriously, keeping close to the side of the building. He couldn't hurry – it was physically impossible – but there was an urgency about him that prevented me from suggesting he should stop and rest. We covered the fifty yards or so to the main entrance more quickly than I would have believed possible in the circumstances.

Once inside the door Fel seemed to relax. He actually

laughed aloud, though the sound came out more like a raucous caw. His colour had returned. His breathing was better. He tried to make light of the whole thing.

'Afraid I'm not as young as I was, Jon.'

'You mean it's a while since you last climbed out of a girl's bedroom window?' I said dryly.

He grinned. 'Sometimes I think you're too sharp for your own good, Jon.'

'And that's unfortunate for me, isn't it?' Now that his appearance no longer frightened me, irritation replaced my concern. 'What do you suggest I do about it?'

He didn't answer at once. Then, as if he had reached a decision, he said: 'We need to have a serious talk, you and me, Jon, but let's get to my room first.'

'All right.'

I didn't care if I sounded ungracious. Of course I was prepared to see him to bed but I had no desire to have a talk with him, serious or otherwise. I was fed up with Fel and his contradictory demands. Either he wanted me to keep out of his affairs or he didn't.

'Come on, Jon. Let's go.'

It was a fair haul up the stairs and along the corridor, through the heavy fire-proof doors. I doubt if Fel would have made it by himself. He was labouring when we reached his room. He sank on to the bed with relief. But he stopped me as I bent to pull off his shoes.

'I can do that. Get me a glass of water, Jon. All that goddam wine has given me a thirst.'

I did as he asked. While I let the water run I heard him kick off his shoes and start to fumble with his clothes. He could have been getting a pill. Certainly when I brought the water I had the impression he was swallowing something. I didn't like to ask him directly. Fel always prided himself on his excellent health.

I said, 'Did you hurt yourself when you landed, Fel?'

'Yeah. I winded myself, I guess, but forget it. I'm okay now.' He shrugged off the incident. 'Sit down, Jon, and let's talk.'

'You'd much better get some rest. Can't we leave it – '

'No!' It was a snarl.

Resigned, I sat and, not bothering to hide my irritation, said, 'Okay, Fel. Go ahead.'

It was still a minute before he spoke and when he did he surprised me. 'I have what you might call a family problem, Jon, and you can be of assistance to me, if you will.'

I stared at him. 'A family problem' was the last thing I had expected. 'Do I have any choice?' I asked bitterly, remembering his previous threats.

And again he surprised me. He didn't answer directly. He said, 'Jon, I helped you when you got into that mess with Darlene Smith. Now I could do with – '

I interrupted him angrily. 'Didn't you even read that letter I sent you? I was framed, Fel. The Smiths framed me so you'd buy them off. Which you did, and I'm grateful. But I wish to hell I could make you – '

'Jon, you were roaring drunk and you don't remember what you did.' Fel shook his head reprovingly. 'The Smiths dropped charges as a personal favour to me. The medical bills, three weeks' vacation in Hawaii, and enough dollars to buy the poor lady a new wardrobe – that's all they ever got out of it. Does that sound like extortion? Would you let your wife be knocked about like that for so little?'

'But – ' I began. Put like that it sounded pretty improbable, but unless Darlene had lied unwittingly it was the only possible explanation of that ghastly night. I knew I hadn't raped her.

'. . . sure I was glad Carol divorced you – you were never right for her, Jon – and with you out of the way I hope eventually she'll marry Bob Verson. So far she's not been too keen and I'm not going to push her even though Bob keeps

76

urging me to – '

'What do you want?' I broke in roughly. 'Whatever it is I'll have to do it, won't I?'

Fel gave a croak of laughter. 'Come now, Jon, you didn't take those threats I made seriously, did you? I was riled. You know I'd never forget you were Paul's father.'

'Thanks!'

It was hopeless. However often I consigned him to Dante's deepest hell I couldn't really hate my ex-father-in-law – Paul's grandpa! His sickly sentiment could make me want to vomit, and often had, but it was genuine. Maximillian Felard loved his family – his wife, his daughter, his grandson, himself, though possibly not in that order.

Reminding myself that Fel was not as other men, I made an effort to get to grips with the immediate problem.

'Tell me what you want me to do,' I said and at least it assuaged my pride that the words came out neither grudgingly nor subserviently.

'I want you to shoot trouble for me till the conference is over.'

I was puzzled. 'Do you mean that literally. What about Verson? Isn't that his job?'

'Sure I mean it literally, but diplomatically too, Jon, for my sake and – and Anna's.'

'Anna? Fräulein Mecklen?'

'Who else? As for Bob – ' Fel hurried on as if embarrassed by the mention of Anna Mecklen – 'Bob Verson's not close family, not yet anyways, and I've told him nothing about all this. Mind you, he's curious, and I can't truly blame him. He knows his future's bound up with mine. He'll travel with me and he'd like it to be up. So he keeps a close eye on me. He'd hate me to do anything one might call foolish, politically, that is.'

Fel stopped and appeared to ruminate. I waited impatiently. Whatever he was trying to tell me he was making

77

very heavy weather of it. I still hadn't got a clue what he was talking about.

'Anna Mecklen is my daughter,' he said abruptly.

'What!'

It was a bombshell. I didn't, couldn't believe it. I heard myself say stupidly, 'Are you sure, Fel?'

'Positive! So please don't start imagining this is some Red plot or the girl's trying to get anything out of me, because it isn't like that. I offered her a raft of dollars and she just laughed at me. No, all Anna wants is a chance to talk with me, to know me a little. Goddam it, that's not so difficult to understand, is it? I am her father.'

'When did you last see her?'

Fel grinned. 'There you go again. You're a cynical sod, Jon. There's no doubt. When the child was born her mother wrote me she was a perfect baby girl except for one blemish, if it could be called a blemish. She had a small strawberry mark on the side of her neck. Anna has just such a mark, hidden by that beautiful hair of hers. Now do you believe it?'

'Sure.' I didn't know what to think.

I didn't like the situation. Even if Anna hadn't been an East German and Comrades Günther and Horst hadn't been in close attendance, it would have been tricky. Fel was the Governor of one of the more important States of the Union, a key man, carrying a lot of clout in Washington, which made him horribly vulnerable to any smear. The whole thing could be political dynamite. But he knew that as well as I did.

'. . . can't pretend I'm particularly proud of my behaviour, but I was young at the time, Jon, younger than you are at this very minute. And the cousins I was staying with in West Berlin – ostensibly to perfect the language – didn't care what I did providing I was no bother to them.

'Gerda was singing nights, in a club, which was where I met her, and we spent all our days together. God, she was a lovely girl.' He smiled sadly, reminiscently. 'I was wild about her. But there was no question of marriage. I was already engaged to Mary and my folk would never have welcomed a night-club singer, leastways not one several years older than me with relatives on the wrong side of the Curtain. And when Gerda told me she was pregnant I just lit out. She wrote a couple of times but I didn't answer except to send her some money when Anna was born, and after that I didn't hear from her again. By then of course I was married to Mary and Carol was on the way, so I was glad to forget the whole thing.'

Fel stopped speaking and waited as if he expected me to make some comment. I didn't know what to say. His story was comparatively commonplace. But the consequences some twenty-odd years later could be far-reaching.

Curious, I said, 'You didn't know that Anna was to be at this conference?'

'No, not till I arrived. There was a letter from Gerda waiting for me. Anna had brought it. She had seen my name on the list of speakers and told her mother she'd like to meet me.'

'And that's really all she wants, Fel? She's not by any chance hoping to defect to the West, is she?'

'No, definitely not. She's devoted to her mother and wouldn't dream of leaving her. She almost didn't come to Norway because Gerda's been unwell recently. Apart from that, why should she want to defect? We haven't talked politics – I don't think they interest her – but she was born in East Germany. It's her home, Jon. Gerda was pretty friendless in the West and managed to get permission to go back across the border and live with her relatives before the baby was born.'

'And subsequently married Herr Mecklen?'

'Yes. Mecklen was a university professor. He was, Anna tells me, a good husband and a very kind step-father. In fact, Gerda only told Anna about me when Mecklen died eighteen

79

months ago. No, Jon,' Fel shook his head in denial of my continued suspicions, 'at the end of the week Anna and I say goodbye. Naturally I'd do whatever I could for her, but she wants nothing from me.'

'Then there's no problem, is there?'

'Only the present one of meeting and talking together. It's not so easy. All these commies are meant to keep an eagle eye on each other while they're in the West, and Günther and Horst scarcely let Anna out of their sight. Tonight was the first time we were able to have a really long chat and even so they interrupted us.'

'Was that why you left through the window?'

'Yeah. We were on the look-out for the Volvo but we didn't see it, and suddenly there's this knock on the door and Günther wanting to know if Anna's okay. She managed to stall him. He didn't come in. But his room's opposite hers and she was afraid he'd be watching. So it seemed best to choose an unorthodox exit.'

Fel yawned hugely. By now he was looking very tired and badly in need of rest. I told him about the breakdowns of the Volvo and my Jag as briefly as I could, shrugging off the coincidence. I was pretty damned tired too.

I said, 'Fel, when are you meeting Anna again?'

'Tomorrow. No, I guess it's already tomorrow. Today – some time. I'll let you know. That is, assuming you're going to shoot trouble for me, because you can refuse. You do realize that, Jon, don't you?' His smile was warm. 'I'm asking you a favour, you understand. I'm not threatening you. No way.'

And it was true. Fel meant what he said. At that point I could have opted out and there would have been no repercussions. I still don't know why I didn't.

The telephone jangled and I started awake. I was in a cold sweat. Seizing the receiver I saw that my bedroom clock said five minutes to ten. I had overslept.

'Hello, Jon. It's Jane speaking.'

'Jane?' I was still drugged with sleep, disoriented, my sub-conscious mind struggling with a dream in which Darlene Smith was both guilty and innocent, was both Anna – and Carol.

'Jane Hamlin, from the Embassy. Who do you think? Do you know dozens of Janes?'

Her tone more than her words roused me, forced me to concentrate. Jane was fraught, which was unusual. I made an effort to placate her, hoping it was the quickest way to discover what had happened, and she swore at me.

'Damn you, Jon. What the hell possessed you to be so stupid? H.E. is absolutely furious. You know he hates to be put in the wrong, especially by a politician, and that bloody Minister made him eat crow. I warn you – ' She stopped short and I heard her say in her official voice, 'Yes, Sir William, I have him on the line. He's waiting to speak to you.'

There was a pause, a click. 'Jon?'

'Yes, sir. Good morning.'

'I'm happy you think so. Personally I can see very little good about it. Maybe when you've given me an explanation of your conduct it'll appear better, but I doubt it.' H.E. spoke quietly, precisely, acidly. 'I'm fully aware you didn't want to go to this Lysebu conference, Jon, but there was no one else to send and it seemed to me to be well within your capabilities to look after the British delegation. However, I gather you prefer to consort with the communists, to spend your time paying court to the beautiful Fräulein from the GDR instead of – '

'The bitch!'

'What did you say?'

'Nothing, sir.'

Jane's warning had been somewhat less than adequate. I hadn't realized that the Minister's trollop would be so vindictive. I had assumed that the Minister, at her urging, had complained about the taxi to Holmenkollen and my general inefficiency in providing him with transport. I hadn't expected to be accused of fraternizing with the East Germans. This was serious.

'As I was saying,' H.E. continued, 'you seem to have neglected your real job and gone to work for the East Germans. May I remind you that it's not they who pay you. To judge from your behaviour last night one might suppose they did. It was disgraceful, Jon, disgraceful and inexcusable. Whatever got into you?'

'Sir, Fräulein Mecklen had been taken ill. Herr Günther was concerned for her and asked me to give him and Herr Horst a lift – '

I was picking my words carefully so as to avoid involving Fel but I need not have bothered. H.E. couldn't have cared less about Fel. He was fixed on me and my 'communist chums' and he really tore me off a strip. Normally a fair and equable man Sir William was in no mood today to be either fair or equable. He was badly riled. The Minister of State might be a buffoon but he was a senior politician, and his complaints – justifiable complaints, it appeared – couldn't be ignored. H.E. had been forced to grovel, which he had not enjoyed, and he held me responsible.

'I appreciate that transport from Holmenkollen late at night was difficult to arrange, Jon, but as I understand it you made absolutely no effort. You didn't order a taxi for the Minister as his PA had requested, and you didn't go back for the other delegates as you'd undertaken to do.'

I ignored the lie about the request for a return taxi. I said, 'My car broke down, sir, and – '

'And you didn't have the courtesy to telephone.'

I said nothing. I was cursing myself. Occupied coping with Fel, I had forgotten my intention to phone Simpson-Brown and warn him I wouldn't be back.

'You will apologize abjectly, Jon, to everyone concerned. And, within the bounds of civility, you will have no more dealings with Mecklen, Horst or Günther.' H.E. punctuated each word separately. 'That's an order. Do you understand?'

I understood, but I wasn't happy about it. Having to apologize didn't bother me. What did worry me was how I was going to keep clear of the East Germans and still help Fel as I had promised.

Swearing under my breath I put down the receiver. This was a hell of a start to the day and, since I was in a bleak mood, I didn't have much hope for the rest of it.

I spent what remained of the morning urging the garage to take rapid action about my car, trying to acquire some breakfast and apologizing to the UK delegates. The results were not particularly successful.

The garage categorically refused to make any promises as to when the Jag would be ready, which put my leave in jeopardy. Mrs Aasen wasn't on duty and the two young Norwegian girls who were laying the tables for lunch giggled nervously, but failed to produce even a cup of coffee. As for my compatriots, their reception of my apologies was mixed, ranging from the kind through the indifferent to the overtly rude. None of this was cheering and, by the time I went in to lunch, I was thoroughly sour.

To add to my annoyance I was immediately buttonholed by Comrade Günther, who insisted on taking me by the arm and drawing me aside. I didn't want to go with him. I was conscious of the Minister standing nearby, and I was sure H.E.'s 'bounds of civility' wouldn't encompass such apparent friendliness with the East Germans. Nevertheless it was difficult to refuse him.

Freeing my arm from his grip as soon as I could, I said brusquely, 'What is it, Herr Günther? I want to have my lunch. I had no breakfast and I'm hungry.'

'It's about your car, Mr Troy, your Jaguar in which you so kindly gave us a lift last night.'

'What about it?'

'I would be interested to know what your garage has said.'

'They've not said a damn thing as yet. They collected the keys from me a mere twenty minutes ago and I imagine that right now they're towing the car into Oslo.'

'Then perhaps I may be of service to you.'

Against my will I hesitated. I didn't like or trust Herr Günther, least of all when he was bearing gifts, but I was passionately interested in anything that might concern the Jag.

I looked at him questioningly. 'How?'

'The firm from whom we rented the Volvo has been most efficient. Not only have they replaced the car, but they took the trouble to telephone me to explain why the first one failed us and I thought you – '

'Herr Günther,' I said impatiently. 'I'm happy for you, but it's most unlikely that your Volvo and my Jaguar developed the same fault on the same night. So, if you'll excuse me . . .'

'No, no! You're wrong, Mr Troy.' He was insistent. 'It *is* mostly likely – because it was vandalism. Someone had poured sand, a great deal of sand, into the Volvo's petrol tank. Since your car was parked next to ours and it also broke down – '

Letting a gesture complete the sentence for him, Günther produced his thin-lipped smile and left me. Sand in the petrol tank? The distance a car would run would depend on how long it took to work into the feed system. Clearly Günther was to be believed about the sand – but vandalism? It was possible, of course. It would explain the coincidence of both cars breaking down, but so would deliberate sabotage. Sabotage seemed to me far more likely.

I resisted the impulse to dash off and phone the garage. Instead, I joined the queue at the smorgasbord. Automatically I collected plate, food, a bottle of beer. And I let my mind play with all the questions. Why had someone attacked Verson and me in the tunnel? Why had the Volvo and the Jag been put out of action? What was Boris Gronski doing at the conference? In spite of Fel's confidences I couldn't come up with any even half-way reasonable answers and at last I abandoned my efforts. For the rest of the meal I surreptitiously studied Anna Mecklen, trying to see some resemblance – apart from colouring – to Fel. I could see none to Carol.

Chapter Six

FEL'S SPEECH WAS scheduled for five o'clock. It was to be one of the more important of the conference. I had known this since reading the material Jane had provided, but it wasn't until I was walking through the tunnel to the main hall where the meeting was to be held that I asked myself what on earth Fel was going to talk about.

It was easy enough to understand why he had come to Lysebu. He was a State Governor and, as H.E. had implied, these days a love affair with the environment was almost a *sine qua non* for any public figure, especially an American. But Fel was no expert on the world's ecology – as far as I knew he had never pretended to be – and what wasn't easy to understand was why, when so many specialists were available and so much expertise, Fel had been invited and had accepted the invitation to be a major speaker.

If others were asking themselves the same question it wasn't keeping them away from the meeting. By the time I arrived the hall was packed. Extra chairs were being brought in but were immediately seized. Someone called my name.

'Jon! Seat for you here.'

'Thanks.'

I hoisted myself on to the window-sill beside Simpson-Brown. It was an excellent place, cool beside an open window and near the door to the tunnel and an easy escape should Fel become too boring. I was grateful to the birdman.

'Order! Order!'

The meeting began. While Fel was being introduced I studied him. He was looking relaxed, but very tired. There were pouches under his eyes and he moved lethargically, as if his limbs were heavy. Admittedly he wasn't a young man and he must have been short on sleep, but he wasn't old either and he had always had the best of health. Remembering last night, I wondered . . .

He began his speech strongly. He was a professional and, in addition, he had this great personal charm – an impossible-to-define charisma. The audience was immediately gripped. Fel was talking of what he knew, economics, making the subject relevant to the world's environmental problems. It was the perfect approach.

I listened, more interested than I would have expected. I no longer queried why Fel had been chosen as a main speaker. As a change from all the specialists he was a brilliant choice. Nevertheless, after a while my attention wandered.

It was a beautiful day, sunny and warm, with the scent of pine trees drifting in through the windows. From my perch on the sill I had a splendid view across the valley. I watched the diminishing dot of a light plane; the red and yellow glint of the Aasen boys' helmets as they endlessly skateboarded on the distant driveway; and, closer, the birds – a cross between thrushes and woodpigeons – scuttling around the grass and clacking like wooden rattles. For me Fel's voice, spiralling lazily to the vaulted ceiling, made an ideal background.

Vaguely I was aware that the door at the back of the hall had opened. Then Fel hesitated in mid-sentence and stopped speaking. And I was startled into the here and now.

'I am so sorry to interrupt. Please forgive me.' It was the attractive Norwegian blonde who acted as receptionist.

'My dear, of course we forgive you. To tell the truth, everyone's delighted I've been silenced.'

Laughter rippled through the room. The girl flushed. She wasn't amused by Fel. Her errand was important. Conscientiously she scanned the sea of faces, all turned in her direction, seeking the person she had come to find. She spoke sharply.

'Fräulein Anna Mecklen is wanted on the telephone. There is a call for her from Germany. It is most urgent. Could Fräulein Mecklen come, please. At once.'

The words, heavy with misfortune, produced a sudden chill silence. The screech of chair legs on the wooden floor as Anna stood up was very loud. Someone coughed, choking off the cough in a handkerchief. It seemed to relieve the tension.

People began to get to their feet, to move back their chairs, to make way for Anna. Murmuring apologies she clambered over legs and pushed past bodies. Everyone was helpful. Everyone was anxious for her. Everyone's attention was focused on her – almost everyone's. Fel wasn't looking at Anna; he was looking at me.

As I met his glance he jerked his head. It could have been a loosening of his shoulder muscles, an involuntary gesture, but I knew it wasn't. Fel was signalling me to go with Anna.

Anna was seated in the middle of a row, and it was taking her a minute or two to reach the door to the tunnel. I slipped from my window-seat and stood, hesitating. As I moved I saw Günther standing also, but in the front of the hall and completely hemmed in by the audience and the extra chairs that filled the aisles. I knew what was in his mind, but he sat down resignedly.

Behind me Simpson-Brown murmured, 'Don't blame you, Jon. If I were your age, I'd be after her too.'

I turned to protest and he laughed at me. I caught sight of the Minister of State sitting beside Miss Carter. I almost got back on the sill and pretended to have been stretching my legs. But Boris Gronski had also risen from his chair strategically placed near the tunnel door. Casually he strolled through it ahead of Anna.

I followed them, shutting the door behind me. The Norwegian receptionist was already clattering up the far steps, the steps where someone had clobbered me on Sunday night. I shivered. It was always cold in the tunnel.

Anna was running. Gronski stepped aside to let her pass, but he lengthened his stride. He seemed to be in a hurry too. And, having no idea why, I hared after them.

By the time I reached the reception hall, Anna was on the telephone, the Norwegian doll was back behind the desk, and Gronski was demonstrating his reason for abandoning Fel's speech by lighting a cigar and drawing the smoke deep into his lungs. I did the best I could. Miming relief at having escaped the boredom of the meeting, I lounged over to a chair and threw myself into it, only to receive a mocking grin from the Russian.

Deliberately I regarded Anna who, oblivious of what was going on around her, was concentrated on her telephone call. She seemed to be doing all the listening while the person on the other end of the line did the talking. If she said anything, and she must have done, it was so low as to be inaudible and, since her head was bent over the receiver, her long hair shrouding her face, even her thoughts were unguessable. Luckily the conversation was comparatively brief.

It ended with shattering abruptness. Anna simply let the receiver fall from her hand and thwack on the counter. Slowly she lifted her head to stare straight in front of her. Tears were meandering down her cheeks. She took two or three steps away from the reception desk, turned in a half circle and crumpled to the ground.

Gronski and I reached her simultaneously. Her breathing was fast and shallow, but her eyelids were fluttering, her colour good. The faint wasn't serious. She was regaining consciousness.

We made her comfortable, straightening her limbs, putting a cushion under her shoulders. Gronski had shouted for brandy but there was none; the centre provided only wine, beer, soft drinks. The Norwegian girl ran to fetch water.

Anna opened her eyes. '*Mein Gott!*' she murmured. '*Nein. Nein. Mein Gott!*' It was an appeal, a prayer.

'What is the matter, Fräulein? Have you received bad news?' Gronski spoke in English.

'Yes. My mother – my mother – ' Anna began, but she couldn't go on. She broke into German, incoherently. 'I should never have come here. It wouldn't have happened if I'd not come. I wouldn't have let her – my dearest mother! What shall I do without her? I knew she was ill. But she would have got better. The doctor said – oh, dear God! Dear God, forgive me.'

The uncomradely appeal to the deity seemed to offend Gronski, who got up from his knees beside Anna, deliberately flicked a speck of dust from his trousers and went to collect his cigar. It was a display of callousness that contradicted the attention he had been giving her and for a second I felt her body tense and sensed the spurt of hatred she fought to suppress.

'Your mother has – died?' the Norwegian girl asked.

'Yes,' Anna said dully. She shook her head at the water that was being offered, and struggled to sit up. 'Please, I – I would like to go to my room.'

'Yes, of course. I understand,' the Norwegian said. There was an angry buzzing from the telephone receiver that was still off its hook. 'But, if you will pardon me. I shouldn't desert my post. Perhaps – Mr Troy?'

Both girls were looking at me and I couldn't refuse. I had no desire to refuse. I helped Anna to her feet. She continued to hold on to my arm but she didn't lean on me. She was

90

controlling herself admirably.

'Thank you.' Her attempt at a smile was pathetic.

With scarcely a word between us, I took her along to her room. She gave me the key and I opened the door for her. Automatically I made to follow her in but she stopped me.

'Please, Mr Troy. I'm grateful, but I'd like to be alone.'

'Is there nothing I can do? No one I can fetch?'

I thought fleetingly of Comrades Günther and Horst and rejected them. Who else was there? Fel?

'Thank you. No. You mustn't worry about me. I shall be all right. It's just – ' She shook her head hopelessly. 'I was devoted to my mother. I would never have left her. Unhappily she has left me. Without her everything is – is now different.'

'I am sorry.'

She didn't give me a chance to say any more. Thanking me again, she pushed me gently from the room and I found myself staring at a closed door.

I waited for Fel. I knew he would come but he took longer than I had expected. I was on my second whisky when he knocked. He didn't waste time on ceremony.

'That goddam meeting! I thought it would never end. The questions went on and on.' He was slightly out of breath. 'What happened, Jon? Was it bad news, do you know? I had a kind of feeling – '

'Anna's mother has died.'

'Anna's mother? You mean Gerda.' Fel sat down heavily on my bed. He was sweating. He didn't seem able to take in what I had said. 'Gerda's dead?'

'Yes.'

I looked at him curiously. I couldn't decide whether he was affected by Frau Mecklen's death or whether he wasn't feeling too well. I poured him a whisky. He drank it in two gulps and held out his glass for a refill.

91

'For Christ's sake, Jon, how? Gerda was sick. She'd had a bad dose of flu and it led to bronchitis, but you don't die from that, these days.' He blotted the sweat from his brow with the back of his hand. 'Goddamit! What happened?'

I told him what I knew. It wasn't really a great deal. But he brooded over it for a full minute.

'Poor child,' he said at last. 'Poor little Anna. I must talk with her, Jon. The trouble is, how am I going to do it. Those goddam commies watch her all the time, and I can't pull another trick like last night. They must never suspect . . .'

He didn't finish the sentence. It wasn't necessary. But I couldn't help wondering, uncharitable though it may have been, if his concern was more for himself than for Anna. He soon made it clear that I, at least, was expendable.

'The swimming pool would be a good place to meet. I'll be there from midnight till one. Let her know that, Jon. She'll come if she can. Incidentally, you'll have to get the key and open it up for us. They lock the place at nine. And you stay around afterwards. We might need someone to run interference. Okay?'

It was certainly not okay, but Fel swept aside my protests. He didn't remind me that I had promised to help him. He merely said he was sure I would manage somehow. I was committed.

I waited until the footsteps and voices outside my room had quietened. By then most people – and I sincerely hoped that included Günther and Horst – had gone down to dinner. I met no one on my way to Anna's room.

She opened the door almost as soon as I knocked. 'Oh, I thought – Herr Günther said he would arrange for a tray to be sent up to me. I'm not hungry but he insisted I should try to eat.'

She spoke very quickly, nervously. Her eyes were red and her mouth pinched with misery. She wasn't pleased to see me. She didn't want company. She began to shut the door.

'Fräulein, please – '

'I'm sorry. I cannot talk now.'

'You must.'

I hadn't meant to sound so aggressive but at any moment Horst was going to come along the corridor with her supper tray. Günther would never let anyone else bring it. And I had no desire to be found here. Hurriedly I gave her Fel's message. 'He knows about my mother? You told him?'

'What little I knew, yes.'

A shadow passed across her face. She shook her head and swallowed. She was having difficuly speaking. Her words emerged in a hoarse whisper.

'I'll tell him tonight – everything. Then he'll have to decide. Do whatever he thinks best.'

She shut the door without bothering to say goodbye and, thankful that whatever decision had to be made would be Fel's responsibility and not mine, I went down to dinner. Predictably I met Horst with Anna's tray, but not until I was at the entrance to the dining-room. My luck seemed to be in at the moment. I hoped it would last.

At approximately eleven-thirty, carrying swimming trunks and a towel, I went downstairs. The night was hot and sticky. Few of the delegates had gone to bed yet. Most of them were sitting around, talking earnestly and drinking beer. Some were strolling about the grounds. It was the perfect time for a swim.

The Norwegian at the reception desk, a male equivalent of the blonde who had been on duty earlier, had other ideas. The bath-house was closed for the day. Anyone wanting to use the pool or have a sauna would have to wait till eight a.m.

It took me at least five minutes to persuade him to change his mind and give me the key. Pretending not to hurry, I set off at a fairly fast walk for the bath-house. This was a two-storey wooden building on the edge of the pine woods, which contained dressing-rooms, showers, saunas and a full-sized Olympic pool. It was ten to twelve by my watch as I unlocked the big double door and let myself in.

I didn't turn on the lights. They weren't essential. There were no windows on the ground floor of the building and the inside was gloomy with long, disturbing shadows, but the gallery above the pool was glassed and provided a fair amount of light. Fel and Anna would be able to see each other.

I expected Fel to arrive well before midnight in case Anna was early, but he didn't and at quarter past the hour, when he still hadn't come, I began to chew my nails. I was sure something had gone wrong. By half past I was so edgy that a sudden, loud, gurgling noise made my heart race, but it was only the recycling system in the pool. I settled down again to wait.

Twenty minutes later Anna arrived, scarcely giving me time to open the door before she was squeezing through. She was breathing hard, as if she had been running. She didn't seem surprised to see me.

'I'm sorry to be late but I didn't want to leave my room until Herr Günther was asleep. Horst is sleeping like a pig. You can hear his snores down the corridor. But Herr Günther's anxious about me and watchful, and it's not long since he put out his light.'

'He didn't follow you?'

'No, no! It's quite safe – but time is precious.' She was peering behind me, into the shadows. 'Where is – Herr Felard?'

'He's not here.'

Instantly she drew back, wary. 'Why not?'

'I don't know. I've been expecting him since midnight.'

I explained how I had got the key, opened the bath-house, waited for Fel. She heard me out without interruption. In fact, she scarcely listened. It was difficult to know how much was getting through to her.

When I stopped speaking she said, in a small voice, 'He's not going to come, is he?'

I glanced at my watch. 'I don't think so. Not now. It's almost one o'clock.'

She leant against the door and shook her head slowly. She looked beaten, defeated, as if all the spirit had gone out of her. I cursed Fel. He was the one who had set up this meeting. Why the hell hadn't he showed?

'Perhaps tomorrow – ' I began.

'When tomorrow? Tomorrow night? That will be too late. Herr Günther has already suggested we should leave the conference early.' Anna put her hands over her face and I could only just hear what she said. 'My poor, dearest mother! Why did she do it? Why? Oh, God – as if I didn't know. It was my fault. If I hadn't told her what I hoped for, prayed for. But it was for both of us. Not for me alone.'

'Anna.'

I took her by the shoulders, held her close, stroked her beautiful, silken hair. And for a long moment she let herself rest against me. Then she pushed me away. Angrily she brushed the tears from her cheeks. Her mood had changed.

'Why didn't he come tonight?' she demanded. 'Was he afraid? Did he guess what I was going to tell him and think I'd make a scene if he refused? Was that why he sent you in his place, to – to placate me?' The questions poured from her.

At last I managed to get a word in. 'Anna, you've got it wrong. Fel intended to be here. I'm certain he did. I can't understand why he isn't, damn him.'

She still wasn't convinced. 'It was his decision. He only had to say yes or no and I would have accepted it. My mother wouldn't have wanted it otherwise, even though – even though – '

95

'Listen, Anna.' I was desperately sorry for her, and I was curious. 'Fel told me about himself and Gerda – your mother – and about you. I promised to help, if I could. But I can't if you talk in riddles. You must trust me. What is this decision?'

'Whether or not I should go and live in America, whether or not I should – defect, as you say.'

I expelled my breath sharply. Fel had said Anna hadn't the slightest desire to defect; she would never leave her mother, her country. He was wrong, or had he been right, but now . . .

'That was what you – you hoped and prayed for?'

'For both of us, yes. The German Democratic Republic is not a good place to live. It's poor and miserable and often frightening. In the United States I could get work at one of the universities. I'm well qualified. I could have earned a large salary. We would have had a nice home, better food, clothes, the things you take for granted – even a little car, perhaps. We could have been very happy – and safe. Of course, we never believed it would really happen, but there was no harm in dreaming.'

Anna spoke simply, as if she had seen the doubts beginning to grow in my mind. She made me ashamed of them. Nevertheless, I was glad it was Fel's problem and not mine.

'And now your mother's died, you hope Fel – '

She interrupted me roughly. 'My mother didn't just – die, Jon. She took her own life. She wanted me to have a chance to go to America, to be free. She knew I wouldn't go without her and she thought I might never have another opportunity like this – being in the West with my – my father to help me, if he was willing. She did it for my sake.'

'Dear Christ!' I said. I was shocked. 'But – how do you know all this?'

'The friend who telephoned me. She found a letter under her door when she got up. She hurried to our apartment but she was too late. The police were already there. My mother

96

had been saving up the sleeping-pills her doctor had pre-
scribed. There was nothing our friend could do, except
telephone me as she had been asked.'

'Poor Anna,' I said gently. 'Your mother must have loved
you very much.'

'Yes, she did.' Anna sighed. 'But she didn't understand. I
have no money, no papers, nothing. I cannot just announce
that I want to defect, not even here in Norway. Herr
Günther would say I was ill, that I was having a nervous
breakdown. There would be a big scene but no one would
want to interfere. I would be taken home, back to the GDR,
in disgrace and it would be worse than it has ever been.'

'Your mother believed that Fel would help you, did she?'

'Yes, but again she didn't understand. He is rich and
powerful, but this isn't his country. Perhaps he's not powerful here. Perhaps he doesn't want to help?' She flung back
her hair and for the first time I saw the little heart-shaped
birthmark on the side of her neck. 'Jon, would you tell him
everything I have told you, please, but say that he must do
what he thinks best and I'll accept whatever he decides.
Make it clear I'm not asking to be recognized as his daughter
– that would be bad for his family, his position – I ask only to
be allowed to live in America, perhaps to meet him
sometimes.'

I looked at her. In spite of her grief she was amazingly
beautiful. I wondered if she was equally innocent, if she
really didn't appreciate the pressure she was putting on Fel,
the moral blackmail. But that was for Fel to decide.

'Of course I'll tell him. And don't worry. God knows why
he didn't come tonight but there must be some good reason.'

'Thank you.'

The whole of our conversation had been conducted
standing just inside the bath-house. We hadn't moved out of
the shadows. Now, thinking she was going to leave, I took a
step towards the door to open it for her, and simultaneously

she stepped forward, colliding with me. Involuntarily I caught her in my arms, her body pressed against me and, as she lifted up her face, our lips brushed.

What happened afterwards was neither casual nor accidental. I experienced an immediate and total physical desire for her. My mouth hardened over hers and our tongues caressed each other, I slid my hand under her skirt. She was warm and damp. She moaned softly as I began to massage her. Her fingers were busy with the buttons of my shirt.

Anna. Anna.

We made love. There was a convenient orange coloured Lilo beside the pool. And it wasn't until she had gone that I thought of Carol, my ex-wife. I didn't know whether to laugh or cry. It was so bloody ironical. This was the first time since the break-up of my marriage that I had had a woman without fantasizing about Carol – and I had been with Fel's other daughter.

To rid myself of painful memories I dived into the pool and swam a slow, lazy length. The water was cool and cleansing and exhilarating. I towelled and dressed.

I still had to discover why Fel hadn't put in an appearance. Having handed in the key at the reception desk, I looked in the lounges and out on the terrace. In spite of the hour there were a few delegates about but Fel was not among them. I decided to try his room.

Comrade Horst wasn't the only delegate with a fine snore. I heard Fel's imitation of an incompetent bassoon player ten yards away. I couldn't believe it. Fel was in fact asleep. Either he had forgotten his rendezvous, which I found impossible to credit, or he had deliberately not shown up. Furious with him I rapped on the door.

'What the hell do you want?'

I swung round. Verson, in dressing-gown and pyjamas, was standing in the doorway of his room opposite. The bruising he had received from his fight in the tunnel on Monday night was beginning to heal but his voice still whistled through the gap in his teeth. I felt no sympathy for him.

'To have a little talk with Fel.'

'At this hour of the morning?'

I glanced at my watch and raised my eyebrows in surprise. 'I've been swimming. I didn't realize it was so – early.'

Verson glared at me. He didn't believe a word of it, in spite of my wet hair and the lingering smell of chlorine from my swim. But he kept his cool. For some unknown reason he even made an effort to be pleasant.

'Okay, but you'll have to postpone your little talk till breakfast. Fel's asleep.'

'I can hear.'

Verson bit off the retort he had been about to make. 'I'll tell him you want to see him. First thing.'

'Thanks.'

I didn't intend to wait on Verson's good offices, but it was pointless to argue with him now – as pointless as to wake Fel out of a heavy sleep and expect him to make a vital decision about Anna. So, with a host of new questions parading through my mind, I went off to bed myself.

Chapter Seven

I WAS AMONGST the late arrivals at breakfast. I had knocked on Fel's door on my way down but there had been no response. There wasn't a sign of him in the dining-room either. I collected food and coffee and took my tray to an unoccupied table. I didn't feel like socializing. Worry was jumping in me. I had been a fool last night. I ought never to have got so involved with Anna; not after H.E. had warned me. And Fel was unpredictable. Why hadn't he –

'Hi!' It was Verson. 'Fel's outside on the terrace. He wants you.'

I was tempted to tell him to stuff Fel but of course I didn't. I finished my coffee and the cheese, and followed him out. Fel was sitting on the parapet, swinging his legs, but as soon as he saw us he slid to the ground and came forward in a big welcoming act.

'Jon, good morning to you and my apologies for standing you up yesterday. I didn't mean to break our date, but I got caught up with Willi Schreiber. He's an important guy in West Germany, as you know, and . . .'

While he talked Fel had taken me by the arm and was leading me down the steps and across the grass. We were going to take a walk together. Verson, obviously primed, had disappeared.

'Fel, why didn't you – ?'

He anticipated the question. 'I just told you, Jon. Willi

100

buttonholed me and I couldn't get away, not without being rude, which I wasn't prepared to be – not to Willi.'

'No, of course not.' I didn't believe him. But what could have kept him away last night? Remembering that heavy breathing and Verson's concern, I wondered if Fel had been unwell.

'Go on, Jon. Tell me. Was Anna there?'

'Yes. She was.' I suppressed my irritation. It was useless being peevish with Fel. But I didn't have to dress it up either. 'It seems Gerda didn't die of bronchitis or its after-effects, as we had assumed. She purposely took an overdose of sleeping-pills. She knew Anna would never leave her but she wanted Anna to be free. She wanted her to defect to the States.'

Abruptly Fel broke his stride and I was half a pace ahead of him when he seized me by the shoulders and swung me round. He pushed his face into mine.

'You must be kidding. If you're not – '

Angrily I shrugged off his grasp. 'I'm not.'

'The bitch!' he said slowly, struggling to believe what I had told him. 'The goddam bitch! I bet she planned this from the beginning, when she found out I'd be at the conference. She meant to screw me real good. Christ, what this could do to my goddam image! It could put paid to – '

'Gerda?'

'Yeah. Gerda. My old playmate, Gerda.' He threw me a sudden, sharp glance. 'You don't think the girl was in on it too, do you, Jon?'

'No!' It was a decisive negative.

I was appalled by his selfishness. He hadn't expressed a single word of regret or sympathy or understanding for the anguish Gerda must have suffered, for what Anna was feeling now. He had thought only of himself, of his 'goddam image'. As if that was so important! He was a State Governor. He wasn't the President.

101

'Fel, she's not asking you to recognize her as your daughter. She only wants help to get to the States.'

'Okay, Jon. Okay. Let's sit down. I've got to give this a hell of a lot of thought.'

We sat on the grass together and, keeping my voice strictly neutral, I said: 'Before you begin to cerebrate, there's one other thing you should know. Anna's prepared to accept whatever you decide. She felt that, for her mother's sake, you had to be told the truth, but she appreciates that it puts you in an embarrassing position, and – '

'Embarrassing position! Christ almighty, it was bad enough to discover I had a commie daughter, but as long as she was happy to stay in the East, to make no demands – what a fool! What a fool!' He groaned aloud. 'I should have guessed it wouldn't be as simple as that.'

For the best part of five minutes we sat in silence, Fel plucking at the turf and worrying his lip between his teeth so that by the time he spoke there was a small pile of loose grass beside his hand and a minute spot of blood on his chin. But he had weathered the storm. He was ready to walk on the water again.

'Well, I guess I don't have any real choice, do I, Jon? In spite of what she says I doubt Anna would be content just to go back home and forget about me. And, after all, she is my daughter; there's no doubt of that. I've got to help her.' He bared his teeth in a smile. 'I'll do my best to arrange for her to go to Britain or Canada for three or four years. After that, we'll just have to see. At least she's not a VIP, thank God. With luck the communists won't blow up her defection into a major scandal. They may even play it down, ignore the whole thing. Who knows?'

It should have been reassuring, but somehow it wasn't. There was no affection in Fel's voice, no warmth in the accompanying grin. I found myself surprisingly disconcerted. And I didn't understand why he considered this preliminary period in the UK or Canada was necessary for Anna. His present term as State Governor would be over in a few months.

'Are you standing for the Governorship again, Fel?'

Fel frowned. He didn't like such bluntness. Then he laughed and gave me a patronizing pat on the back, which I resented. He didn't answer the question.

He said gently: 'Jon, politics apart, I can't afford to have this business of Anna foul my nest. No way! You must understand that. There's my dear Mary to consider, and Carol, and the rest of the family. Some of them are important people, and their lives wouldn't take kindly to the publicity of an unexpected relative from behind the Iron Curtain.'

'No. I suppose not.'

It was a valid argument. I couldn't have explained why it didn't ring altogether true. Perhaps Fel sounded too persuasive, too much like a salesman selling a product he knew to be faulty. But there were more immediate things to worry about. I dismissed my doubts.

'Fel, the conference ends the day after tomorrow. If Anna's not to go back to East Germany, something'll have to be laid on pretty rapidly.'

Using my shoulder as a support Fel got to his feet. 'I realize that, and it's no mean problem. It's a hell of a pity – '

'What?'

'Jon, don't take offence. What I was going to say was – it's a pity you aren't Bob Verson. He'd be just the man to deal with this kind of situation.'

I stood up. 'I'd be happy for him to be my guest.'

'No, no. I don't want him in on it, not if it can be avoided.' Fel was quick to correct any wrong impression he might have given me. 'As I told you, Bob's got a vested interest in my affairs and that's fine, but it's never advisable to let anyone have too much of a – a claim on you.'

103

Fel had chosen his words carefully, but their meaning was very clear. For 'claim' substitute 'hold' and the next step could be 'blackmail', politely called 'pressure'. Fel knew his Robert F. Verson. Presumably he also knew me. I wasn't sure whether to take it as a compliment (he considered me too honourable) or an insult (he considered me too stupid), but evidently he assumed I would never be a threat to him.

'Listen, Jon. I've had an idea.' Fel picked up the stitches of our conversation. 'I've a friend in the US Embassy here who owes me. He and his wife have a *hutte* on one of the fjords, where they go in the summer. If Anna could hole up with them for a week or two until the excitement's died down and I've had time to make some long-term plans for her, it could be ideal. I'll go and call him now, arrange to lunch. But I'm sure he won't refuse. Jon, you tell Anna everything's fine and she's to be ready to disappear tomorrow. Okay?'

He was striding off, not waiting for me to agree or disagree, intent on achieving his purpose. I didn't try to stop him. I was thinking about Anna. I was wondering just how far she was prepared to trust Fel – and me. Which reminded me of my own involvement. And I made a promise to myself that, whatever happened, come Saturday I was going on leave to the peace and quiet of Brittany.

I was thankful when the day was done and I could retreat to my room. I lay on the bed, half awake, half asleep. It had been a day of non-events but one which amply justified the dictum that if anything can go wrong, it will – altogether an unfriendly day.

I had been caught by Comrade Günther knocking on Anna's door and had hurriedly to make up a spurious excuse about wanting to know how she was and offering my sympathy. My second attempt to speak to her – at lunch where she appeared, red-eyed and wan – had been partially successful but had been observed by the codfish eyes of the

Minister. And I could see myself being asked some awkward questions when Anna decamped tomorrow.

If she did. By late afternoon Fel still hadn't succeeded in reaching his chum at the US Embassy. However, though Verson was at dinner, Fel was not and his car was missing from its parking place. I could only hope that he had at last managed to make contact. Expecting Fel to come and tell me what he had organized, I hadn't undressed. I thought about the following day. In the morning I was due to go into Oslo to collect the Jag. Günther had been right; they had found sand in the petrol tank. I sighed. The bill would be horrific. But at least I would be able to collect a bottle of whisky while I was in the town. It was the final blow that I was now out of Scotch.

The one bright spot in the day had been the half-hour I had spent with the Aasen boys. Olav had insisted on teaching me to skateboard and had been delighted when I proved such an apt pupil. I grinned sleepily – they were nice kids – I hadn't had the heart to tell them I had a nine-year-old nephew who considered himself an expert . . .

The next thing I remember was rain drizzling on my face. It was cool and pleasant and gentle. I lifted up my head so as to enjoy it more. But without warning it became needle sharp, piercing, achingly cold. Bells were clanging. I sat up in bed. I was wide awake.

It wasn't raining. The water was spraying from the sprinkler rose in the middle of the ceiling. The bells were a warning, an alarm. I coughed and coughed again. Smoke was ghosting under the door. Fire. And the whole place was wood – walls, ceilings, floors.

Without conscious thought I was on my feet, slipping into my shoes, seizing my jacket. I checked my pockets for wallet, passport, keys. They were all there. I was wearing my watch, my signet ring, my cuff links. I was still fully dressed. The windows were shut.

It was well under a minute since I had been so rudely wakened. I edged open the door. Smoke billowed into the room, getting into my throat and making my eyes sting. Hurriedly I slammed the door again.

I wasn't afraid. There was no real danger. Fel had demonstrated that it wasn't difficult to climb out on to the sill and drop to the grass below. But I had once been trapped in a hotel fire in the south of France and it wasn't a happy memory. My adrenalin was pumping fast. I ran some water into the wash-basin, soaked a towel, wrung it out and wound it around the lower part of my face.

I did the same with the other two towels. Above the alarm bells I could hear indiscriminate noises, shouts, people calling to each other. Even if the fire was small and confined to this wing of the building there would probably be some panic, the odd inexplicable accident, the need for help. I opened the door again, and slid into the corridor.

The acrid smoke made my eyes water. It was impossible to keep them open. Slit-eyed, I groped my way along. More and more delegates were debouching into the corridor, coughing and choking. I gave up my wet towels to two of the more elderly. Others went back for their own. Everyone was very well behaved. There was in fact no panic, except momentarily when someone slipped going down the steps that led from the fire exit and fell, causing a mini-avalanche of bodies. Even then we were lucky. Except for a twisted ankle no one was hurt.

And what a relief to get outside. I unwound the towel from my face, dabbed at my sore eyes and took great gulps of warm night air. It tasted wonderful. I looked at the people milling round on the grass, some of them dressed, some of them in pyjamas and dressing-gowns, others in a motley of garments – the first things to come to hand.

106

Deciding to check on the UK delegates, I discovered that Simpson-Brown had forestalled me. In a scarlet track-suit, his wispy grey hair standing on end, he had organized the Brits and was prepared to organize everyone else. He greeted me with enthusiasm.

'Ah, there you are, Jon. Splendid! But we're still one missing. Sir Theodore's charming PA hasn't put in an appearance yet and – '

'I'm afraid Miss Carter mightn't have heard the alarm, that she might still be in her room.'

I swung round on the Minister. The pompous little man was in his night clothes, a heavy silk gown over pyjamas. I noticed that he had remembered to knot a scarf at his throat and pick up his briefcase – though not, apparently, to check on his girl-friend. But she must have heard the alarm bell and felt the water from the sprinkler, unless . . .

'Does she usually sleep very heavily?'

It was an innocent question, but he went puce in the face, his eyes bulged and a spot of spittle appeared at the corner of his mouth. I didn't wait for him to stop spluttering.

'I'll try and find her,' I said to Simpson-Brown.

'Good!' He grinned at me. 'You go ahead, Jon, but mind yourself. In the meantime I'll make sure that everyone else is present and accounted for. I've a list of the delegates with me, which is lucky, seeing that our Norwegian hosts seem to be more concerned with their famous conference centre than with us.'

Simpson-Brown gestured cynically to where the towering figure of Mr Aasen was standing and pointing up to various parts of the second floor. It was obvious he was giving instructions to the group around him about locating the source of the fire and containing it. Even as we looked he led half of them into the building, while the other half ran off to enter by another door.

I thought Simpson-Brown's criticism somewhat unfair.

Smoke was now clouding through some windows that had been left open. An occasional flicker of flame could be seen. The smell of burning was growing stronger. I had no idea where the fire brigade would come from or how long it would take to get here, but clearly immediate action was necessary if the fire was to be controlled.

Of course the birdman was partially right; a member of the centre's staff should have been appointed to check that everyone had got out of the place safely. But first things first. The delegates were all able-bodied adults who had had ample warning and opportunity to save themselves. As for the Minister's trollop, she was the last person I would have expected to need rescuing.

I loped over to the door through which Aasen had gone and had my hand outstretched to open it when I heard my name shouted. Verson, waving desperately, was pushing his way through the delegates towards me. When he reached me, he seized me by the arm. He was breathing hard as if he had been running.

'Jon, what's going on? Where's Fel?'

'Fire. Didn't you know? Where've you been?'

'I couldn't sleep and went for a walk. I was up in the woods when I saw everyone – where's Fel, Jon?' Verson nearly shook me. 'He's not out there, in that crowd. Where is he?'

'I don't know. He went out to dinner.'

'Don't be bloody stupid. He was back hours ago. Goddamit, it's past three! He must be still in bed. Come on!'

Verson thrust past me into the building and I followed him. There was no point in arguing. I thought that Fel was probably with Anna somewhere. I hadn't seen her outside. Admittedly there were a lot of people milling around and I hadn't been thinking of her, but I remembered noticing Boris Gronski and Willi Schreiber and that pleasant Frenchman . . . Anyway, I had a missing Brit to find.

Verson took the steps two at a time and ran along the corridor. The alarm bells had stopped ringing but water continued to spray from the ceiling roses. The smoke was thin, scarcely noticeable – this wasn't the way I had come before – until we pushed through one of the fire doors, when it drove us back, black, acrid, choking smoke.

'Christ!' Verson said. 'How do we get in there?'

It was a rhetorical question, but I had a partial answer. The wet towel that had protected me before was still around my neck. Verson held it stretched while I slit it with my pocket-knife. It made two fairly adequate face-masks.

'The third door to the left. If it's locked, we'll have to break it down. Ready?'

'Sure. Go ahead.'

Break down the door? It was madness. I didn't believe Fel was anywhere near his room. But somehow Verson had impressed me with the vital importance of finding him and by now I was almost as anxious as he was.

In the event, however, we burst into the room against the minimum of resistance – the duvet from the bed. It had been pushed against the bottom of the door and had kept out ninety per cent of the smoke. This, added to the fact that the windows were wide open, had perhaps saved Fel's life.

Fel was lying on the floor in a crumpled heap. His jaw had fallen open and he was breathing stertorously. Verson, who had dropped to his knees beside him, lifted a stricken face to me. He was as putty-coloured as Fel but he didn't have that frightening blue-white line around the mouth. His voice was icily calm.

'Lean out of the window, Jon. Fall out if necessary. But attract the attention of those buggers down there. Fel needs a doctor, an ambulance. He must be taken to hospital – at once.'

Equally appalled by Fel's appearance, I seized a towel, waved and shouted from the window. As most people were staring up at the building it was only moments before some of them came running.

'Get a doctor and an ambulance. Quick as you can. Governor Felard has had – '

A hand closed round my ankle, the nails bit into my skin and I winced with the pain. Jerking backwards into the room I hit my head on the window-frame and swore.

'An accident!' Verson emphasized, grinding at my ankle. 'Smoke inhalation. Tell them.'

'Rot you!' I kicked myself free, viciously pleased when my shoe made contact with the side of Verson's already battered face. But I repeated what he had said to those beneath the window. 'Accident. Smoke inhalation.'

'For God's sake, hurry!' Verson prompted.

'For God's sake, hurry!' Involuntarily I reproduced Verson's words and his urgency.

'Okay! Right away!'

A Dane, whom I knew to speak Norwegian, waved and ran off purposefully. At the same time two fire trucks, a car and an ambulance came screaming over the brow of the hill and down the driveway. Someone was shouting at me.

'Troy! Troy, have you found Miss Carter? Is she all right?'

'Christ!' I had completely forgotten the bloody girl. 'Yes, Sir Theodore. Don't – don't worry! Everything's under control.'

'What was that? What did you say, Troy?'

I didn't bother to answer. Half falling over Verson where he was attending to Fel I started for the door, once again winding a towel around my head.

'Where the hell are you going?' Verson demanded.

'To see if the girl's in her room – my Minister's PA. I'll be back in a minute. Fel will be okay. An ambulance has just arrived.'

'Keep the bloody smoke out!'

Verson practically pushed me into the corridor and

110

slammed the door behind me. Disoriented, I set off in the wrong direction. I had to retrace my steps and, when I got to the right place, the door was locked. I banged furiously on the panel and rattled the handle. There was no answer. But anyone who had slept through the alarm bells and the sprinklers could presumably sleep through anything.

I tried to listen. It was useless. There were too many other noises outside and inside the building. I was tempted to leave it at that – the fumes were beginning to nauseate me – but, much as I disliked the little bitch, the possibility that she was lying unconscious on the floor like Fel prevented me.

I had to get into her room somehow. Unluckily the corridor was an impossible width, too narrow to allow me to take a good run at the door, too wide to offer me any purchase to kick it in. Standing sideways on, I hurled my weight against the panelling. Nothing happened.

I tried again. At my fourth or fifth attempt the lock gave, the door burst open and I fell into the room on an already badly bruised shoulder. Half dazed, I picked myself up and stumbled over to the bed.

The Minister's Personal Assistant was flat on her back on top of the duvet. She was naked – peculiarly naked because all her pubic hair had been shaved – but she was alive. Her breasts, beautifully shaped with small, bright pink nipples, moved rhythmically up and down as she breathed. I felt no desire for her whatsoever.

I shook her hard. She smiled foolishly, murmured 'Darling' and pursed her lips for a kiss. I would have dearly loved to slap her, but there wasn't time. I wrapped her in a towelling robe that had by chance been well soaked by the sprinkler and would protect her from smoke and fumes. Then I hoisted her over my shoulder in a fireman's lift. I made no attempt to be gentle.

She was heavier than she looked and I only just made it back to Fel's room. I dumped her on the bed, ran to the open window and, tearing the towel from around my head, took great gulps of air into my lungs.

'What the hell?' Verson was furious. He leapt to his feet and once more blocked up the bottom of the door.

'She – she was in her room – drugged, I think – sleeping-pills.' I shrugged impatiently. 'Does it matter?'

'Get her dressed, Jon.'

'What?'

'Dressed. Get her into that robe. Make her look respectable.'

For a moment I stared. I was still breathing quickly. Respectable? He couldn't mean it. He had to be joking. Robert F. Verson was no prude. I laughed and he swore at me.

My jaw must have dropped. Verson was serious. His face was a bruised, lop-sided mask of determination. And outside the window the top of a ladder crashed against the sill, startling us both.

'Quick! Help me!'

Verson spoke through his teeth. His lips scarcely moved. But there was a viciousness about his words that startled me and he was already busy making the Minister's trollop decent – though why he should bother, I had no idea.

Chapter Eight

THE FIRE WASN'T really serious. It had started in a walk-in cupboard where cleaning materials were stored and where, regrettably, the cleaners sometimes smoked. It was in here that bottles of fluid had exploded, giving off nauseous fumes and the black smoke that had caused most of the damage.

There were three casualties, a Swede with a sprained ankle, Fel and the little bitch I had rescued. The Swede refused to go to hospital. The other two, both unconscious, were removed in the ambulance. Verson went with them, but no one else. The Minister, having assured himself that Miss Carter was getting adequate attention, had discreetly withdrawn, and it was quite plain I wasn't needed.

I was more use at the centre. There was a lot of clearing up and reorganizing to be done. Though the damage was restricted to one wing of the main building the rooms there were unusable, many of them filthy dirty, all of them wet. Their former occupants had to be found accommodation, possessions had to be moved, clothes dried and aired. The actual cleaning was left until the day staff arrived, but in the meantime the Norwegians were thankful for any help they could get.

I was transferring the belongings of one of the older delegates to another room when Anna found me. Her anxious, pinched face was a reproach. For the last while I had scarcely given her a thought.

'Fel – how is he, Jon? Was he badly hurt?'

113

'No. No. He wasn't hurt at all.' I tried to reassure her. 'He's suffering from smoke inhalation. They'll give him oxygen, I imagine, and he'll be fine.'

'How soon?'

'I don't really know. Later today – or tomorrow.' I remembered Fel lying on the floor and the way Verson had reacted. I felt suddenly cold. 'Anna, Fel did talk to you yesterday evening, didn't he? Tell you what he had arranged for you.'

'No. He told me nothing. I haven't spoken to him. It was you who said at lunchtime that everything would be all right. But it isn't, is it?'

I forced myself to smile at her. 'It's going to be. Fel's been making arrangements. He intends you to stay with friends of his who have a *hutte* not too far from here. That's until he can get you out of the country to – to the States. So, cheer up! It'll work out.'

It was very near the truth and should have deceived her, but it didn't. A few outright lies might have been better. She shook her head miserably.

'How can it, when he's in hospital? If only he'd not gone to rescue that rude, unpleasant girl it might have been different, but – '

'It was nothing to do with her. Fel didn't – '

'I overheard Herr Verson tell Sir Theodore that Governor Felard saved her life. It's sad it should be at my expense.'

'You overheard Verson – ' I couldn't believe it. 'You must have misunderstood.'

'Anna! Anna, what are you doing?' Günther came striding along the corridor, interrupting us. 'You should be in your room, resting, my dear, even if you can't sleep.'

'That's just what I was telling the Fräulein, Herr Günther,' I said equably. 'She mustn't worry about – other people. All is under control. All will be well.'

But I wasn't as optimistic as I sounded.

Immediately after breakfast I set off for the nearest tram stop. My first priority was to visit the hospital and speak to Fel, alone. Once I knew what he had laid on with his friend at the US Embassy – and, I told myself, he must have organized something; he wouldn't have returned to the conference centre and gone calmly to bed otherwise – I would have to help Anna get safely away from Comrades Günther and Horst. The rest, thank God, wouldn't be up to me. In fact, it would be better if I didn't know where she had gone.

'Mr Troy! Good morning, Mr Troy.'

Trotting down the hill behind me came Willi Schreiber, his big head held stiffly as if he were using it to keep his balance. I stopped and waited for him. I had no desire for his company – I had too much on my mind – but I couldn't be rude to the little man.

'You – you walk very fast, Mr Troy.' He was breathing quickly. 'It's your long legs, no doubt.'

Altering my pace to suit his, I grinned at him. 'You're not attending this morning's meetings, Herr Schreiber?'

'No. Alas, no. I felt I must go into Oslo, to the hospital, to enquire after my old friend Governor Felard.' He smiled up at me. 'I assume that's where you too are going, Mr Troy. You and your former father-in-law are still close. Isn't that so?'

I nodded agreement, wondering at his excessive concern. I would have expected him to enquire after Fel, perhaps to make a personal telephone call to the hospital, but not to cut what I happened to know was one of the last important sessions of the conference in order to make this tedious, inconvenient trip into the city. And for what? Did he hope to talk to Fel – about something vital? Anna? I told myself I was being absurdly suspicious.

'Poor Maximillian,' Willi Schreiber said, 'how he must be regretting his eagerness to be a speaker on the world's environmental problems.'

'Eagerness?'

I wasn't really interested. I could hear a tram coming and I didn't want to miss it. Involuntarily I lengthened my stride. Herr Schreiber began to run beside me.

'Yes, indeed. We politicians are all the same, Mr Troy. We think always of what will bring in votes at home and make our names better known abroad.'

I laughed. 'Even when you're at the top.'

'Then more than ever. There is invariably another summit to be attained.'

But right now what we needed to attain was the tram, which had clanked through the rock cutting and was standing at the station. This was no time for a philosophical discussion of the political animal. I sprinted across the tracks, Herr Schreiber panting after me. Together we boarded the tram, paid our kroner and sank on to the nearest seats. We had made it.

'If you will pardon me, Mr Troy. My room was untouched by the fire but it was an interrupted night.'

The little man folded his arms, closed his eyes and was instantly asleep. I envied him. The tram was noisy and stopped frequently. The seats were uncomfortable. The gradient inconveniently steep. To have said that my night had been interrupted would have been an understatement, but I couldn't even doze. I was glad when we reached the terminus.

From there to the hospital was a brief walk. Herr Schreiber, who had woken as easily as he had gone to sleep, chatted about the conference and the need for global co-operation to prevent pollution. I half listened, making the right noises. My mind was on Fel – and Anna.

I would have to let Schreiber go first, but I hoped he wouldn't stay too long with the invalid. The tram trip had been slower than I had expected. The best part of the morning was already spent and there was still the Jag to be collected. Depending on what Fel had to say, wheels might be indispensable.

But we had reached the hospital. Schreiber swept through the doors and up to the enquiry desk. I followed meekly, hoping I could turn his authority to my advantage.

'We would like to see Governor Maximillian Felard. I am Herr Willi Schreiber. And this,' he added as an afterthought, 'is Mr Jonathan Troy.'

'If you will wait a moment, please.'

The girl spoke very fast into the telephone. I didn't understand the Norwegian but I could guess what she was saying. I caught the names of Felard, Troy, Schreiber – and Verson. She asked us to take a seat; a nurse was on her way. And, indeed, a nurse appeared almost at once.

'Please come with me, Mr Troy.'

Embarrassed, I looked doubtfully at Schreiber. He was, after all, an important man, many years my senior and an old friend of Fel's. There must have been some misunderstanding. I was sure Fel would have given him precedence over me – unless, of course, he had something very urgent to tell me about Anna.

Reluctantly I said, 'Perhaps we should go together, sir.'

The nurse shook her head as the West German stood up. 'Mr Troy. Only Mr Troy.'

Willi Schreiber shrugged resignedly and sat down again. 'You go ahead, Mr Troy, but please to let Maximillian know I am here.'

Assuring him that I would, I followed the nurse to the lift and along a wide, green corridor. Things were working out better than I had expected. If only Fel's embassy chum hadn't let him down –

'This is the room, Mr Troy.' The nurse knocked, opened the door and gestured to me to go in.

'Thank you.'

Two strides into the room and I stopped, disappointed and

angry. In the bed, propped up by pillows and looking very decorative, was Miss bloody Carter. Verson was sprawled in the armchair beside her. Fel wasn't there.

'Come in, Jon,' Verson said, grinning at my disgusted expression.

'I want to see Fel.'

'But you can't. He's given strict orders. He doesn't wish to see anyone. He inhaled more of the smoke and fumes than we realized and he's feeling rotten.'

'How rotten?'

'Oh, not too bad really. He should be okay tomorrow or the next day.'

I thought of Anna; that would be too late. I had to talk to Fel today – if it were possible. He could be too ill to talk. Verson was obviously hiding something. I could always tell when he was putting up a smokescreen around Fel. The difficulty was to know why.

I would have pleaded with him if I had thought it would do any good, but I was sure it wouldn't. The alternative was to threaten.

I said, 'Verson, I've something extremely important to discuss with Fel. If he discovers you've needlessly obstructed me there'll be all hell to pay, and you'll pay it.'

He shook his head. 'The answer's still no. Sorry, Jon.'

'All right.' I was surprised he should express even careless regret. 'Incidentally, Will Schreiber's downstairs. You won't be able to fob him off so lightly.'

'Then it's up to you, Jon, but don't make a big thing of it. That would be bad for the image.' He grinned at me conspiratorially. 'Tell him the Governor's sleeping.'

The bloody image again! Fel was ill and Verson didn't want the fact broadcast. It was bad news for Anna.

'Poor old boy!'

I had been aware of the other fire casualty, lying there tan-cheeked and healthy, her blonde hair fluffed out around her pert little face. But the comment startled me. Was she referring to Schreiber or Fel? Neither of them would have appreciated the description.

'Whom do you mean?'

'Governor Felard. Who else?'

'I wouldn't know. You could have meant your boss, Sir Theodore,' I said sweetly. 'He's about the same age as the Governor.'

She glared at me. 'Piss off, Troy. This is my room and no one invited you in here.' She turned to Verson. 'Tell him to piss off.'

Verson pushed himself out of the armchair. 'I'll see you to the elevator, Jon.'

'Thanks,' I said sarcastically.

'A charming girl,' he said as he shut the door behind us. 'Full of gratitude to Fel for having saved her life last night.'

I looked at him in amazement. 'Then it was you who started that story?'

'Sure. Great publicity.'

'But doesn't she remember?'

'Not a goddam thing. Evidently her period started and she took some pills her doctor had given her. They were supposed to knock her out for ten hours, which they certainly did.' He laughed. 'You don't mind not getting the credit for rescuing her, surely, Jon.'

'I wish I'd left her to roast,' I said bitterly, and a patient who was being wheeled from the lift stared at me oddly.

Verson, suddenly serious again, laid a restraining hand on my arm. 'Remember. Play it cool with Willi Schreiber and I'll let Fel know you want to see him the minute he's up to it. You'll be at the conference centre?'

'When I've collected my car, yes.'

'Okay, then.'

I wasn't going to get any more out of Verson and waiting around for him to contact me was a dismal prospect, even if

119

he was to be trusted. The alternative was to make a big noise about being Fel's son-in-law and appeal to the hospital authorities behind Verson's back. But I had scarcely debouched into the lobby when it became apparent that this wouldn't work either.

To my surprise Schreiber was confronting a tall, fair woman with a white, heavily starched, inverted chimney-pot on her head. He introduced her as the hospital's senior matron, saying: 'Mr Troy, I hear you have not been permitted to visit Maximillian. They say no one can see him.' He turned to the matron: 'Madam, this is Mr Jonathan Troy of the British Embassy. He is Governor Felard's son-in-law and surely has a right as a relative to – '

Two cold blue eyes regarded me. 'The doctor's not at present in the hospital, Mr Troy, but his instructions were definite. No visitors. Governor Felard must rest today.'

'It's extremely important,' I began urgently. 'A family matter that – '

'I'm sorry.' She didn't sound in the least sorry. 'Good morning, gentlemen.' Nodding a brisk dismissal, she turned away and left us.

What the hell was I going to do about Anna now? Adjusting my stride to the West German's as we walked down the street together, I chewed over the problem. Unless and until I could speak to Fel it seemed to me insoluble. There was no one else I could appeal to – fleetingly I thought of H.E. and imagined his reaction if I appeared at the Embassy with an East German refugee – no one who was capable of helping. Fel had been explicit that Verson was to know nothing of the situation.

'Mr Troy, there's a pleasant-looking café over there. May I offer you a drink?' Schreiber said, suddenly breaking into my thoughts.

'Thank you very much, but – '

'Since I can't talk to Maximillian himself, it's essential I should talk to you – as his son-in-law.' It was a flat statement.

I would have preferred to be on my own, to go and collect my car, but half an hour wasn't going to make a lot of difference, and 'essential' was a strong word. I prayed that the little man wasn't going to produce another problem for me.

'His ex-son-in-law,' I corrected gently. 'And, since you press me, thank you, sir. I'd love a beer.'

We crossed the road to the café and sat ourselves at a table outside within sight of the Royal Palace. It was full of tourists, most of them young and with camping paraphernalia stacked beside them, but the service was good. The beer came quickly. And Schreiber began to talk.

'Mr Troy, I'm leaving for Bonn this afternoon – I'm not staying for the end of the conference – so I've no chance of seeing Maximillian tomorrow, but I hope you will and I hope you'll give him a – a message from me. In my position, as I'm sure you'll appreciate, I get to know a lot of things, personal secrets, business secrets, government secrets. Recently I was told such a secret. I can't vouch for the truth of it. I tried to check, but without success, though there have been some pointers. This is one of the reasons why I haven't mentioned it to Maximillian already. But he is an old friend, and last night I decided he had a right to know.' He paused, frowning. 'What do you know of Boris Gronski, Mr Troy?'

The question took me by surprise. 'I – er – met him in Washington. He was a Minister at the Soviet Embassy.' I hesitated. Schreiber almost certainly had more information on Gronski than I did. 'It was believed that his diplomatic status was only a cover, and that really he's a top – ' I stopped and grinned apologetically. 'But then, sir, I'm sure you're better informed about that sort of thing than I am.'

'He's a dangerous man,' the West German said sombrely. 'I was disturbed to see him at the conference. Mr Troy, you must warn Maximillian – ' He broke off. '*Mein Gott*, if only I had some real knowledge.'

'Sir?' I wished he would come to the point.

'To be blunt, it is possible – and I stress the word possible as opposed to probable – that there exists a communist plot to destroy Governor Felard.'

'To destroy Fel? Do you mean – assassinate him? But – but why?'

'Why not?' Schreiber was impatient. 'He's a powerful man and a bitter opponent of all the East stands for. He's always treated so-called détente with the contempt it deserves. In any case, you don't have to kill a man to destroy him.'

'And you believe Boris Gronski's involved?'

'I don't know for sure, Mr Troy. I know very little, as I've said. But I do know that Maximillian should be warned. So will you tell him, please, just what I have told you – as soon as you can and in the strictest confidence.'

'Yes, of course.'

'And you'll say nothing about this to anyone else, not even to your ambassador?'

'No!' The monosyllable didn't seem to satisfy him and I felt compelled to add, 'You have my word, Herr Schreiber.'

'That's good enough for me. Thank you, Mr Troy.'

Solemnly Schreiber offered me his hand and, straightening out an incipient grin, I shook it. I didn't know what to make of his story. It appeared to be little more than a rumour, but obviously he took it seriously. At any rate I could be thankful it had nothing to do with Anna.

'May I offer you the other half?'

I glanced at my watch. 'Thank you, no, Herr Schreiber. If you'll excuse me, I really must go and collect my car.'

This time the little man didn't insist and I left him and set off for the garage. But, in spite of what the mechanic had said on the phone, the Jag wasn't ready. I hung around, went to have a sandwich, came back, argued, but it was no use. I had to be content with a promise that the car would be delivered to me the following morning.

Compared with my failure to talk to Fel, this was a minor matter, but somehow it was the last straw. Feeling irritable and frustrated I returned to the conference centre as I had come, by tram. The best part of the day had been wasted and nothing achieved.

The evening was no improvement. Naturally, Verson didn't telephone and, whenever I rang the hospital, he wasn't available. The official bulletin on Fel continued to be bland and unmeaning. I tried to have a word with Anna but during supper Günther and Horst were constantly beside her and I daren't go to her room afterwards. Anyway I had nothing new to tell her. She already knew that the conference was to end at noon tomorrow, and her chances of staying in the West under Fel's auspices were growing slim.

A violent bang against the door of my room woke me. I had gone to bed, prepared for a white night, but I had been tired, horribly tired. Within seconds my eyelids were drooping and I was asleep. Now I was fully awake, every nerve taut.

'What are you doing, Fräulein?'

'Nothing, Herr Günther, nothing. I knocked my suitcase on the wall. It was an accident.'

'Come along then, and be quiet. Remember it's four a.m. Do you want to wake everyone?'

The angry German conversation ceased and footsteps retreated along the corridor. I sat up in bed. My heart was thudding against my ribs. The unnecessary noise. The loud mention of a suitcase. It hadn't been an accident. Anna wanted me to know that she and the comrades were leaving the centre, though God alone knew what she expected I could do about it.

Certainly I hadn't the faintest idea. Nevertheless, I was already out of bed and pulling on some clothes. I sprinted along the corridor, through the fire door and down the stairs into the reception hall. The place was deserted.

123

I opened the main door and went outside, looking casually around me as if I were contemplating some exceptionally early, pre-breakfast exercise. I knew where Horst always parked the Volvo and, as I expected, there he was, busy stowing luggage into the boot. Günther and Anna were about to get into the car.

I began to walk down the steps, not hurrying, but as if I had just seen them and was coming across to say goodbye. In fact, it was a waste of my acting ability. They were much too occupied to notice me.

An ugly quarrel appeared to have spurted up between Günther and Anna and, while I choked on my amazement, Günther suddenly lifted his hand and struck Anna viciously across the face. Anticipating the blow she dodged to one side and managed to avoid its full force, though it threw her off balance. She started to run back towards the building, but she stumbled, almost fell. Not that she ever had a chance.

I was much too far away to be of any use and Horst was very quick on his feet for such a big man. He caught Anna before she had gone ten yards, scooped her up and air-lifted her back to the Volvo. Then, with a brutal contempt, he tossed her on to its rear seat.

Involuntarily I had begun to run towards the parking area. Horst, hardly waiting for Günther to get in beside Anna, had flung himself behind the wheel and was accelerating up the drive. I delayed to try the doors of each of the three parked cars but they were all locked, so I cut across the grass. I was in sight of the Aasens' lodge when the Volvo turned on to the road.

It did occur to me to wake the Aasens and ask to borrow their car but it would have meant explanations, excuses, a waste of time, and they might have refused; it was a new car – according to young Olav, the first brand-new car they had ever owned – and safely locked in their garage. If it had been easily available I would have taken it.

At that moment I would have taken anything that was readily available. It was imperative to get to the airport before the East Germans flew out. I was assuming they were making for Fornebu, though no planes took off so early. They would have to wait and, while they waited, I would have to organize some sort of showdown to ensure that Anna didn't fly out with them.

Previously, at the back of my mind had been the belief that even if she had to return behind the Iron Curtain now, she would get another chance to escape, and the next time Fel would be prepared. But the violence that Günther had shown her and the reaction to her abortive attempt to run had demonstrated that this was no longer true.

Somehow Anna had betrayed herself. Günther had discovered she wanted to defect and, once the East Germans got her home, they would soon know why. It wasn't only Anna who was at risk. It was Fel, and what Fel stood for. If they chose, the communists could use his daughter as a propaganda vehicle. I could imagine Boris Gronski as the supposedly impartial observer. He would make his version of Anna's story stink to high heaven. I had to prevent that from happening, if it were at all possible.

As I ran past the Aasens' lodge I stopped abruptly. The gleam of chrome had caught my eye. There was a bicycle leaning against the side of the house; Mr Aasen used it to get around the grounds. I hadn't ridden a bike since I was a kid but surely it was something one never forgot. At any rate, it was my only chance. I was already breathing hard. I could never make it on my own two feet.

In retrospect I suppose it was a mad idea. But it could have worked, if the hill hadn't been so steep, if I had been a more adept cyclist, if I hadn't met a Dormobile at the very place I had picked up Verson three nights ago. Up till then I had been going pretty well. I had wobbled about a lot but I hadn't actually fallen off. As a result I had become over-bold, over

125

confident – and fatalistic.

I heard the Dormobile's driver change gear and saw a glint of headlights through the trees, but I had no time for defensive action. I was in the middle of the road. He was taking the bend too widely. I did the only thing I could and threw myself sideways. I was a fraction of a second too late.

The front bumper caught me on the shoulder and tossed me out of the way. The bicycle continued on its course under the Dormobile. I distinctly heard the wheels scrunching it to pieces. And my last thought before I hit the tarmac was not of Anna but of Mr Aasen. I would have to buy him a new bicycle.

PART TWO

Chapter One

THE WORLD ENVIRONMENT CONFERENCE was over. I couldn't have been more thankful. In the inside of a week I had been slugged by some unknown, threatened by both Fel and Verson, received an undeserved rocket from H.E., had my car sabotaged and almost ended my life in a very undignified road accident. In addition, my bank balance had gone even further into the red. I had increased my debts by the price of the Minister's taxi to Holmenkollen, an enormous repair bill from the garage, recompense to the owners of the Dormobile I had scraped, and a cheque to Mr Aasen.

And for what? Having got myself involved in what could yet become an East-West scandal, I had failed to achieve the one thing that was important. I hadn't prevented Comrades Günther and Horst taking Anna back to East Germany. Admittedly it wasn't altogether my fault, but the result was the same. Not even the fact that I was going on leave tonight relieved my gloom.

I deposited Simpson-Brown and two other Brits at Fornebu. At least my Jag had been returned and was running splendidly. As I drove away from the airport I saw the Minister of State helping his girl-friend out of an American staff car. Verson, on Fel's behalf, was putting her still more in his debt – and probably earning me another rebuke from my ambassador, which I could ill afford.

I sighed. I was already so unpopular with H.E. that God

help me when he heard of last night's cycling fiasco. And he would hear; there was little doubt of that.

Despite my protests which they had only partially understood, the couple in the Dormobile had driven me back to the conference centre. They were local people making an early start on their holiday and, having recognized the delegate's badge pinned to my lapel, they were determined to return me to my friends and equally determined to explain what had happened in their own language, so that no blame should attach to them. As a result I had come in for a lot of badinage from my fellow delegates and had been forced to plead an ill-considered bet. But that wouldn't satisfy H.E. He would think I had gone mad. In my present sour mood I was inclined to agree with him.

From the airport I went to the Embassy to pick up my mail. On a Saturday afternoon in midsummer the place was dead, which suited me; the last thing I wanted was to have to give Duncan a blow-by-blow account of the conference. Then, unwillingly, I drove to the hospital. I wasn't looking forward to my meeting with Fel.

As it turned out I needn't have worried. I was told that Governor Felard was much better but regrettably at the moment in a deep sleep; Mr Verson was not in the hospital. However, as if to assure me that none of this was polite fiction, it was suggested I should return the following morning. Disguising my relief – I intended to be on my way to Brittany tomorrow – I asked if I might leave a note.

Paper and an envelope were provided and I retired to a table, to chew the end of my pen. It wasn't an easy note to write. I didn't want Fel to be in any doubt as to what had happened, but Verson wouldn't respect the sealed envelope. I had to be circumspect. Eventually I came up with:

'Dear Fel, I'm sorry the fire caused such an unfortunate ending to the week, but everyone has gone home now and

130

there's nothing to be done about it. One can only hope that the final results of the conference won't be too disastrous. Meanwhile I'm glad to hear you're recovering. I'm off on leave today so I won't be seeing you again. Best wishes. Jon.'

I reread what I had written. There was a lot left unsaid, but I couldn't think of a way to tell Fel any more – especially the fact that Anna's East German keepers seemed to know of her plan to defect – not without informing Verson at the same time.

I addressed the envelope and was about to lick the flap when I remembered Willi Schreiber. Quickly I added a postscript: 'Herr Schreiber sends his regards and said you should take more care of yourself. He seemed to think that you are accident-prone these days.' That was as explicit as I dared to be. I could only hope that, if there was some truth in the little man's story, Fel would take it as a warning. Anyway, that was the best I could do.

It was with an enormous sense of freedom that I let the hospital doors swing shut behind me and ran down the steps to the car. As far as I was concerned the whole bitter episode was now over. There was nothing more I could do about it. Deliberately I turned my thoughts to Brittany and my leave. I was feeling in much better form when I arrived at the block of flats where I lived.

The janitor accosted me in the hall while I was waiting for the lift. 'Mr Troy, I hope it's okay, but you're not here and your wife says – '

'My wife?'

His English was considerably better than my Norwegian but I couldn't take in what he was trying to tell me. For some obscure reason – it had to be connected with Fel; perhaps she had been in England and Verson had phoned her – Carol was in Oslo, upstairs, in my flat. My heart thumped unevenly as the lift carried me upwards and I walked along the corridor. I

131

inserted the key in the door with difficulty. My hand was shaking.

'Hello, darling.'

The casual greeting, a mask for my true feelings, ended in a croak. It wasn't Carol who was slowly getting up from the sofa. It was Fräulein Anna Mecklen of the GDR.

'Anna!' I exclaimed. 'What the hell are you doing here?'

It wasn't the most welcoming of greetings and as soon as I had spoken I regretted the words. Anna looked tired, bedraggled and woebegone. I think she had been asleep and I had woken her.

'Jon, I'm sorry. I didn't know where else to go. Günther had found out somehow and I was afraid – '

'Found out what? About you and Fel?'

She swallowed as if she couldn't speak and shook her head. Then the words came out in a rush. 'No – no, not that. Just that I was hoping – planning to defect. He threatened me. He said he'd see to it when we got home that I'd lose my job at the university, all my privileges. He said I must have been a subversive for years, I'd go to prison and when I came out – if I came out – I'd be an old woman.'

I looked at Anna in despair. My emotions had changed in such rapid succession, disappointment at not finding Carol, shock that the East German girl was actually here in my living-room, anger at my enforced involvement with her, pity, apprehension at the possible consequences. My mind, like a bee, buzzed from thought to thought and settled on none. I felt shattered.

It was Anna, collapsing into tears, who steadied me, brought me to my senses. I poured her a brandy and held her while she sipped it. In a minute or two she stopped crying. She even managed a lop-sided smile.

'I'm sorry, Jon. I shouldn't have come to you, should I? But there was no one else.'

I ignored the question. 'Tell me what happened, after

132

you left the centre. I did try to follow you but – without success.'

'We went to the airport. I was desperate – I knew I had to escape somehow – but I pretended to be subdued and obedient. I asked if I might go to the cloakroom – Günther could hardly refuse – and I climbed out of the lavatory window and ran. I was very lucky. A man offered me a lift into the town. He dropped me near what he said were the parliament buildings. I didn't know what to do. I had no money, no papers, and it was so early. The people who were around looked at me oddly. I walked, pretending I had somewhere to go, and I sat on a bench for a while. Eventually I went into a public lavatory and put my hair up under a neckerchief I'd been wearing and – '

'Why on earth?' I was puzzled.

'So that I wouldn't be so easy to recognize. You see, I didn't think Günther would catch the plane without me. I thought he'd reclaim the Volvo and come searching for me. I was terribly afraid, Jon, but I was trying to be logical. I looked up your address in a telephone book – I had the map of Oslo that the Norwegians gave all the delegates – and I set off to find you, if I could, to ask you – beg you to help me get in touch with my – my father. I did think of going to the hospital myself but – ' She broke off. 'Jon, you will help me, won't you?'

'Yes, of course. How can I refuse?'

If she appreciated the irony of my words, she gave no hint. She thanked me gravely as if I were doing her an enormous favour when, in fact, I had no choice. I couldn't turn her out into the street. I had to help her. I forced myself to think.

The first thing was to see Fel. And this time neither the starched matron nor Verson was going to keep me away from him, whether he was sleeping or not. Thank God he was feeling better. If he had been seriously ill . . .

'Jon, could I make myself a cup of tea? Please. I've had

133

nothing all day except the brandy you gave me and it's made me sort of light-headed.'

'Yes, of course. Help yourself to anything you want. There are some biscuits.' It sounded as inadequate as it was. Poor Anna. 'I'm going to the hospital now. Depending on what Fel says, I'll bring something in.'

I stopped abruptly, realizing what I had just said, how much I was committed, and bit back an oath. I should have been packing, getting ready to load the Jag. But it wasn't on. There was no point in fooling myself. I wasn't going to catch the ferry tonight. My leave was, at best, postponed. I refused to think about the worst.

Grim and determined, I started once more for the hospital. The same receptionist was on duty and I expected her to be surprised at my return, but it annoyed me that she was shaking her head before I had even opened my mouth.

'I'm sorry, Mr Troy.'

'So am I,' I said, 'because I'm going to have to insist. I have to see Governor Felard immediately.'

'But that's not possible.'

'Is Mr Verson in the hospital?'

'No. He has gone. They have both gone. Which is why it is impossible for you to see Governor Felard, as I would have explained if you had given me the opportunity, Mr Troy.'

'Gone? But – but where?'

'I've no idea, Mr Troy. They didn't leave a forwarding address. There was no need. When Mr Verson returned to the hospital this afternoon, shortly after you had called, he merely said that Governor Felard would be checking out. The doctor was happy to give his permission. Mr Verson settled the account. And they left. It was as simple as that.'

I must have looked stricken because she gave me a bright smile and added, 'I didn't forget your note, Mr Troy. I gave it to Mr Verson the moment he came in.'

'My note,' I repeated stupidly.

134

I thought with horror of what I had written. If Fel had interpreted the message correctly he would believe that Anna was back in East Germany and that I had gone on leave. Which meant he was most unlikely to try to get in touch with me. And by now he could be on his way home to the States in the belief that nothing could be done about the situation, except pray there would be no scandal to tarnish his image.

'Is there anyone who might know where I could contact Governor Felard? His nurse, perhaps? Or the doctor. Please ask. It's most terribly important.'

My urgency got through to her and she went to a great deal of trouble, but it wasn't any use. It seemed that Fel, escorted by Verson, had left the hospital in a chauffeur-driven car. It was assumed they had gone to the airport, though no one knew for sure. I said thank you and goodbye.

I drove to the US Embassy. The duty officer was equally helpful. He confirmed that the car had come from the official pool and he telephoned the driver, who had gone off duty. The driver said he had dropped Governor Felard and Mr Verson at the airport but no, he had no idea which flight they were catching.

From the US Embassy I went to Fornebu, where I explained my problem to a helpful clerk. While he checked the passenger lists for me, I casually picked up a copy of the *International Herald Tribune* that someone had left on a table. And the headline leapt at me: 'Gov. Felard Saved My Life'. The piece was short, but the picture of the Minister's PA, decently wrapped in her robe as Verson had insisted, was worth a thousand words.

I was grinning wryly when the clerk returned to say that the names of Felard and Verson didn't appear on any of the regular passenger lists, and my grin faded. Only one possibility remained – a private plane and, after further enquiries, I established that a commercially owned executive jet had landed, boarded two passengers, and taken off again almost at once. The pilot had filed a flight plan for Eastleigh, England, but the names of the passengers were unknown. I had to assume they had been Fel and Verson, his ever-watchful aide.

Indeed, I made a whole lot of assumptions, such as – Fel wouldn't have flown into Southampton if he had intended to return to the States at once; therefore he was probably staying with friends or business associates somewhere in the south of England. It didn't help much. After a fortune spent on international dialling I located the pilot to whom it had been merely a dull, routine job, and Mary Felard who, if she knew anything about Fel's whereabouts, was not prepared to be helpful.

And late that night, as I lay in bed beside the beautiful East German defector, I wondered what on earth I was going to do. H.E. wouldn't act in Anna's case, I was sure – even with a long explanation which wasn't mine to give. Any other embassy – the American or the Canadian – would inevitably involve publicity, the last thing Fel would want, or Anna either if she were to join him. Eventually I had to accept it. I had no choice. For the present the responsibility for the Fräulein was mine alone.

'Wake up, Jon!' It was an urgent whisper. Anna was shaking me. 'There's someone in the apartment.'

Reluctantly I opened my eyes. Half fuddled with sleep, I had to adjust to my surroundings. I wasn't at the conference centre as I had expected. I was in the bedroom of my Oslo flat. The sun was streaming through the window on to Anna's lovely naked body, and light footsteps were tapping across the wooden floor of the living-room, into the passage, the bathroom and back to the living-room.

'Jane,' I said, unaware that I spoke aloud. I had forgotten

that Jane had a key, that she was going to borrow the flat.

'Your girl-friend?' Anna asked.

'No! Someone from the Embassy. Keep quiet!' I whispered savagely.

The last thing I wanted was for Jane to come into the bedroom and see Anna. I was determined not to involve her with the East German. Violently I jack-knifed out of bed, threw the duvet over Anna, covered myself with a robe and, yawning prodigiously, went into the living-room.

'Good morning, Jane.'

'Jon! Oh, God – you nearly made me jump out of my skin. I thought – '

'I'm sorry. My plans went awry. There was a fire at the conference centre and – '

'Yes, I know. Your father-in-law rescued Sir Theodore's PA. It was in the paper. Are they all right?'

'Fine, but the admin held me up, and I didn't manage to get away on time.'

Jane nodded her understanding. 'You'll be going today then?'

I stammered a negative and saw her eyes widen with surprise. My mind blanked. I could think of no acceptable reason why I should suddenly decide not to go on leave. But what was I to do with Anna?

I heard myself say, 'Monday. There'll be less traffic and it'll be altogether more comfortable than at the weekend. That'll be okay for you and your cousin, won't it?'

'Yes, of course, Jon. Thanks.'

It took me another five minutes to ease her out of the flat and on my return to the bedroom I found Anna in a state of nerves. She made no excuse for having listened to my conversation with Jane. She exploded into questions.

'Who is that girl? You said it was someone from the Embassy. The British Embassy? And what is her cousin that you have to leave your apartment for him? You said Monday

137

– where am I to go on Monday? What am I to do? You must tell me, Jon.'

'For God's sake, be quiet a minute and let me think,' I snapped.

Anna wasn't the only one who was on edge. I was fraught myself. Jane's appearance had shaken me, and the fact that I had forgotten about her cousin made me wonder what else I had failed to take into account.

'Jon, please, what is happening on Monday?'

'That's the really vital question,' I said dryly. 'The rest are immaterial.'

'And so?'

I made up my mind. 'Anna, it's going to take some while for me to get in touch with Fel and for him to organize things for you. It could take a week, two weeks, even more, and it's not feasible for you to stay here that amount of time.'

'Why not? Because of that girl?'

'Partly. She's my ambassador's secretary and she's also my neighbour. She already thinks it odd I've not gone on leave. She knows how keen I was to get to my house in Brittany. Then there's the janitor, who believes you're my wife and the woman who comes in to clean the place. It's simply not safe, Anna. On Monday we must go.'

'But where, Jon? Where?' Suddenly she was bright with hope. 'To England?'

'Regrettably, no. It would be more convenient since Fel might be there, but I don't have anywhere you could stay. Besides, we'd have to fly in, and immigration's strict at Heathrow. France is a much better bet. I've a cottage – a small house, really – in Brittany and . . .'

Anna didn't want to go to France, but the more I elaborated the idea the more sensible it seemed to me. The house was isolated. No one came near it. Even the farmer and his wife never intruded on me but always waited for an invitation. It was a perfect place for Anna to stay until I could get hold of Fel. And it ought not to be too difficult to reach. Unless they were making specific checks, frontier officials were apt to wave on cars with diplomatic plates after only a cursory glance at passports.

'Let me look at your passport,' I said.

'Jon, I don't have it. Herr Günther kept all the passports and the money, everything. I have the clothes I was wearing when I fled, and a few bits and pieces in my shoulder bag. Nothing else.'

I swore. Clothes were unimportant. Necessities, like a toothbrush, could be readily bought. But without some kind of travel document Anna was not going to get to France or anywhere else.

'I'm sorry,' she said despondently. 'You've tried so hard to help me, Jon, but it's no use, is it?'

I forced myself to grin at her. In for a penny, in for a pound. I couldn't abandon her now.

'It's possible I might be able to get you a British passport,' I said slowly.

'Jon, could you really?' Her face lit with joy like a child's at the sight of a birthday cake. 'That would be wonderful.'

The duty officer regarded me with a raised eyebrow. 'This is an excess of zeal, Jon. Given up your leave for love of your work?'

'Not on your life. I'll be setting off on Monday. But I've been having some trouble with my car.'

I told him about the sand in the petrol tank, blaming the incident on vandals. I wanted him relaxed, incurious. What I was about to do was crazy but there didn't seem to be any alternative.

'. . . so I thought I'd come in and finish off all sorts of odds and ends,' I said apologetically. 'Can I help myself to the keys?'

'Of course. Take what you like.'

He lifted his legs, banged his feet on the desk and yawned. He was bored. Nothing of any interest was going to happen on a midsummer weekend in the British Embassy in Oslo. I sympathized. In his place I would have felt the same.

I took the keys to my office and the file room, and also those for the consular division and its cabinets. 'Thanks a lot. I shan't be long.' With a cheerful wave and a promise to have a drink with him before lunch I went along to my room.

Having created a confusion of papers on my desk, I sat and glowered at them – and my watch. I allowed myself five minutes. They were a long five minutes. I could feel the Embassy around me, sun-warmed, silent compared with its weekday activity, sleepy. I wasn't deceived. Apart from the duty officer who might suddenly decide he would like a chat, the security guard would be making his rounds and, Sunday or not, one of my colleagues might come in to do a little work. I couldn't count on being undisturbed.

When the five minutes were up, I tucked a file under my arm and walked purposefully along the corridor. Avoiding the lift, I took to the stairs. I was praying hard.

Earlier in my career I had done my consular training and a stint in the consular department in London. Even here in Oslo I had helped out when the consuls were overloaded with lost passports and other problems of the itinerant young. In any case, in a small embassy like this, and given access to the cabinet containing the blank books and the necessary stamps, the procedure was quite simple. Take a blank book, glue in the photograph, emboss it appropriately and fill in the details by hand. The problems would arise when and if the numbered blank was missed. Depending on the enthusiasm of the staff and the efficiency with which they investigated its absence, either I could go to gaol, or the loss would be put down to clerical error. Anyway, by that time I hoped my efforts would have served their purpose.

I let myself into the consular office. The first thing was to find a suitable photograph – one that would resemble Anna enough to pass for her, not as she really looked but as we could make her appear. If I couldn't find one she would have to go to a photographer's tomorrow, and that would be complicated. I could hardly postpone my leave again, and pull a similar trick to get the keys.

I rifled through the drawer of processed passport applications, each with its duplicate photograph. Almost immediately I struck gold – a picture of a woman, aged about thirty-five, with fair hair coiled on top of her head, her unlined face expressionless. I doubt if it did her justice, and it was a caricature of what Anna might expect to be in ten years' time, but it was the best I could hope for.

The next step was the passport itself. I turned to the cabinet that contained the hard-covered, dark blue, gilt-crested books, and took one from the middle of the pile, feeling slightly stupid as I wrapped a handkerchief round my hand to do so. The glue for the photograph was at hand, and so was the embossing machine. I added the rubber stamp 'British Subject, Citizen of the United Kingdom and Colonies', and locked up quickly. The details I could fill in at leisure in my flat.

It seemed I had achieved my object. Everything was ready for our trip to Brittany tomorrow.

Chapter Two

'Merci, monsieur – mademoiselle.'

The officer saluted smartly. To one side of him a civilian, wearing a very English-looking tweed hat that didn't disguise the fact he was a security man, dismissed us with a scarcely perceptible bow, but his eyes, I noticed, lingered admiringly on Anna. I started the engine and the car edged forward. The barrier came up.

'Merci, messieurs,' I called easily.

We drove into France. I restrained myself from pushing the accelerator to the floorboard. I drove sedately, speeding up only when we were out of sight of the frontier post. My mouth was dry. My shirt was sticking to my back. I eased the collar away from my neck.

'What was that he said about my passport?' Anna asked.

'He said, *"très triste"*. He meant it didn't do you justice.'

'How nice of him.' She smiled.

Throughout the journey Anna had been calm and un-flustered. Much of the time she had dozed. She had offered to drive but, as she had no licence, I didn't dare let her. When she wasn't sleeping she looked idly out of the window at the passing scenery. She asked few questions. She wasn't interested in the countries we were driving through. Her curiosity seemed to be reserved for the United States, and particularly the Felards. It wasn't a subject that appealed to me at the moment.

I was feeling distinctly jaded. In the best of circumstances it was a long drive from Oslo to Val-en-Bretagne. Even though it was autoroute most of the way and I knew a couple of good inns where the meals were superb and the beds comfortable, I was always glad to arrive. On this trip I had bought food for picnics and we had slept in the car which had been exhausting, but worth it if we could travel more or less unnoticed.

There had been no mention of Anna's disappearance on Norwegian radio before we left Oslo, or on any of the stations I could get en route, and nothing in any newspaper I had seen. Certainly it wasn't making front-page news. Perhaps Fel had been right, perhaps the East Germans would play it cool. But I didn't believe Comrade Günther would return home without making some effort to trace Anna, and I intended to take every possible precaution.

So far we had been lucky. The weather had been good. The Jag had gone well. There had been no trouble at any of the border posts, but my heart was still knocking against my ribs as I drove down the autoroute. The French had been looking for someone or something. The DST man with his incongruous little hat had been there on a tip-off and, though he wasn't after Anna, thank God, he would remember her, and me and the car – if the occasion arose. I wondered what the penalty was for forging a British passport and aiding and abetting a communist defector to become an illegal immigrant.

'Well, here we are in France,' Anna said and sighed. She was still wishing we could have gone to the UK. 'Jon.' She put her hand on my thigh. 'Couldn't we have a proper meal tonight? To celebrate our safe arrival?'

Safe? I wouldn't feel safe until I was in my own house in the depths of Brittany, until I had located Fel, until I was rid of Anna. She was a beautiful woman. She excited me physically. I was desperately sorry for her. But I did not

143

delude myself. I wasn't in love with her, and I wouldn't consider my future well lost for her.

'Jon, what's the matter? You're not angry with me again, are you? I haven't done something else stupid?'

'No, of course not. I'm tired, Anna. That's all.'

I heard the tartness in my voice. I wished she hadn't reminded me. On the Monday morning before we left Oslo I had gone into the town to buy a few things she needed and, returning, had found her on the telephone. She was speaking German. It had only been a Norwegian who had got a wrong number, but I was furious. It could have been Günther checking up on me, and Anna had been mad to answer the telephone. Nevertheless, losing my temper had served no purpose.

'I'm sorry,' I said. 'We'll stop at the first Jacques Borel wc come to and have a good dinner.' I grinned at her. 'Then I must get some sleep. Otherwise I'll be driving off the road.'

She squeezed my thigh. 'That will be wonderful, Jon. Thank you. Thank you, *mein liebling*, for everything. I'll make it up to you one day, I promise.'

It was late morning when we reached Dinan. A hot meal and several hours' sleep in the carpark before we continued our journey had put me in better shape. And it was a glorious day, white clouds scudding across a deep blue sky, the sun dazzling bright, the river sparkling. My spirits rose.

I turned the Jag into a petrol station and eased up to the pumps. The proprietor came out to serve me. I had stopped here before on several occasions and he recognized me, welcomed me – but his eyes were for Anna. It was a reminder that I had been careless, that I couldn't afford to relax my guard.

While the tank was being filled and the oil checked I collected the keys for the wash-rooms and showed Anna where to go. I hurried to be the first to return to the car. I

144

didn't want the garage man starting a conversation with her. I didn't particularly want to talk to him myself. I walked up and down, stretching my legs, waiting for him to finish, waiting for Anna to reappear.

He came trotting over to me. He was a short, rotund man with a beer belly. I imagined him with a short, fat wife and six happy children. He had struck me as being a cheerful sort of guy, but at the moment his face was creased with concern. He looked like a woebegone basset hound.

'Yes. What is it?' His anxiety had communicated itself to me. I was sure something had gone terribly wrong with the car. 'What's happened?'

'Monsieur.' He took a deep breath and exhaled, blowing garlic at me. 'You are a diplomat, no? British?'

'Yes.' I hadn't expected this approach.

'And you have enemies perhaps, foreign agents?'

'What makes you ask that?' I had nearly laughed but just in time I remembered Günther and Horst. The Frenchman's remark wasn't as wild as it seemed.

He took a step closer to me and I backed away as the wave of garlic enveloped me. He grinned nervously. His teeth were very white against his tan. He was excited.

'Monsieur, I must tell you. There is a funny little black box under the rear bumper of your car. I noticed it when I dropped the cap of the petrol tank and bent to pick it up. Could it be something dangerous? We have read in the papers of so many . . .' In his agitation he made to put his hand on my arm, but withdrew it quickly when he saw the grease on his fingers. 'Come, monsieur, I will show you.'

'All right,' I said quickly. He had shaken me. I admit it.

'Here, monsieur.' The proprietor led me to the back of the Jag.

I slid my hand under the bumper and felt cautiously. It seemed much too small for any bomb I had ever read of, much more like something electronic. It even appeared to

145

have a short piece of metal extending from it, like the antenna of a transistor. I hesitated. Should I get the authorities? Surely a bomb or anything of that kind would have gone off by now if it had been planted in Norway. An investigation by the police was the last thing I wanted.

I pulled nervously. The object was clearly attached to the metal bumper by a magnet. Out in the light it was a small sealed plastic box about an inch square, with a rod extending about two inches from one end. It looked something like the bugs I had been shown during security briefings when I joined the FCO, but who could hope to eavesdrop on conversations in a car from a bug planted outside? It could only be some kind of homing device to transmit a signal and enable me to be followed. But this was James Bond country; I gathered that in real life there were innumerable difficulties about using these things on crowded highways, unless the followers had a general idea of the ultimate destination of the car they were pursuing.

'That's too small to be a bomb,' said the garage man. 'Shall we try a screwdriver, monsieur?'

I was about to reply when I saw Anna approaching across the forecourt of the service station. I pushed away the screwdriver and thrust the box at him.

'Take it. I'll be with you in a moment.' I gave him a conspiratorial grin. 'We mustn't frighten mademoiselle, must we?'

'But no, monsieur. No, indeed.'

He trotted off, his big belly wobbling, and I turned to greet Anna. To my annoyance she had unpinned her hair and it was lying about her shoulders in a shining bronze fall. I couldn't blame the Frenchman for stumbling over his feet as he caught sight of her. But I did blame Anna. He was going to remember us anyway. She needn't have made it easier for him.

Biting back an angry remark, I opened the car door for her

146

and said, 'Just going to get my change.'

The Frenchman had placed the box on the counter and was attacking it gently with his screwdriver. He was being watched, somewhat nervously, by a bright-eyed brunette whom I took to be his daughter, but whom he introduced as his wife.

'May I, monsieur?'

'Of course,' I agreed, shaking hands with madame. 'The honour is yours, monsieur.'

I had scarcely finished speaking when he turned the screwdriver and the box sprang apart with a sharp crack. His wife screamed. Bits of plastic and tiny electronic components sprayed into the air.

'*Voila, monsieur!*' He was triumphant.

'Yes,' I said bleakly.

It was difficult to accept the absurd. Yet the absurd had happened. Someone had actually planted a homing device on my car. It had to be Günther or Horst, but the East Germans must have known how ineffectual such a gadget was. And, if they had been so sure Anna was with me, why hadn't they taken some more direct action before? It didn't make sense.

The Frenchman was watching me eagerly. For all his fondness for melodrama he wasn't a fool. It was too late now for me to pass everything off as a joke. I had to take him into my confidence, or pretend to.

Feeling like a character in a bad play, I said: 'I'm most grateful to you, monsieur and madame, most grateful. Of course you'll understand I can offer you no explanation, but I assure you I have French interests at heart as well as British – and, therefore, I'm convinced you will forget everything that has happened this morning.'

'We have already forgotten, monsieur. We haven't seen you, or your beautiful companion.'

I was satisfied with that. They would remember very quickly if French security started making enquiries, but they

147

wouldn't help anyone else. And luckily I had never mentioned Val-en-Bretagne.

Val-en-Bretagne. How can I describe it? It might qualify as a town, if the adjudicator were generous. It was a community of houses, a single street of shops with the usual cafés, one hotel, an ancient monastery with a church attached, a mayor, a mill, an apology for a river, a handful of artists and, fortunately, only a few discriminating tourists. To me it was a dear, familiar place. I had known it all my life.

If Val-en-Bretagne was off the beaten track, the house that my great-grandfather had built over a hundred years ago was remote. Nine kilometres outside the little town, through a network of deep-cut lanes and past the farm that my family had once owned, I swung the Jag so sharply on to a dirt track that Anna gasped. A bumpy ride of a quarter mile brought us to the house, a long low whitewashed building, its shutters fast, sleeping in the sunshine.

'It's lovely,' Anna said, 'but lonely, so far from anywhere. Do you have a telephone?'

'Good God, no.' I laughed. 'That's the last thing I've ever wanted here. Except perhaps on this occasion.'

I unlocked the front door and led her into the hall. Inside it was warm and smelt of furniture polish. I opened the windows and flung back the shutters. Sun streamed on to the carpet and, in spite of the problem of Anna, it was good to be home.

I showed her the upstairs. We went into the bedroom together and, though she was with me, when I saw the old brass bedstead I thought longingly, not of sex, but of sleep, twelve whole uninterrupted hours of sleep. First, however, we had to unpack and have a meal, and talk. Anna was impatient. She hadn't pressed me during the trip, perhaps because I had been short-tempered. Now she was determined to know what I had in mind.

148

'I'm sorry to spoil your leave, Jon, but I have got to find my father. It's nice here, and you say no one ever comes to the house without warning. But I can't stay here indefinitely. What happens when you have to return to your office?' She made a hopeless gesture. 'Please. You do understand? I must find him – or rather you must find him for me. Quickly. There have been so many wasted days already.'

'Tomorrow,' I promised.

Anna was right. Now that she was reasonably safe – and I was fairly confident that her fellow-countrymen wouldn't have followed us further than Dinan – the top priority once more was to get hold of Fel. And surely that ought not to be impossible. He was too important a man to disappear for long.

'And what will you do tomorrow?' Anna demanded.

'Drive into Val-en-Bretagne and do some long-distance telephoning from the hotel there. I know the owner. He'll let me use his private phone.'

'Who will you call? You tried in Oslo but it was no use.'

'Mary Felard will have heard from Fel by this time. I'll try her again.' I had thought of Carol, but I doubted if she would speak to me and I didn't want to mention her to Anna. 'Then there's the State Governor's Office. They must be in touch with him and with Verson. They'll relay a message.'

'Why didn't you telephone them before?'

There were ice crystals in her voice and I hesitated. It required an effort to check the angry retort I yearned to make. I had to remind myself what a strain she was under.

'At the weekend no one who could have helped me would have been at his desk, and during the drive down it wasn't possible to wait for a call to be returned,' I explained gently. Not giving her a chance to comment, I continued, 'I also intend to phone a newspaper friend of mine in London. He has a lot of contacts and should be able to trace Fel if he's still in England. But it will take time.'

149

Anna shook her head as if to rid herself of black thoughts that I could only guess at. 'Jon, I'm sorry, truly sorry. Of course you're right. Tomorrow you'll do all these things and, please God, you'll discover where he is.' She came across to me and kissed me on the mouth. 'Let's go to bed now.'

We slept late and it was noon when I left the house. I went first to the farm. It was important to behave as I always did. I sat at the scrubbed wooden table in the kitchen, while Madame Le Blanc produced a bottle of wine and one of the children went in search of their father. When Le Blanc arrived we discussed some business, and he brought up the subject of the sagging floor in my living-room.

'You have seen it yourself, monsieur. You appreciate the position. Something must be done and done soon, or the job could grow out of proportion.'

'I'll have to think about it.'

'But, monsieur, it's not wise to delay.'

Puzzled, he looked at his wife for support. He didn't understand. Usually I was amenable to his suggestions. And this was essential. What's more he knew I knew it. But when Madame Le Blanc, who had been watching me closely, said nothing, he contented himself with a Gallic shrug.

'As you wish, monsieur. As you wish.'

They would debate the matter when I had gone. Possibly madame might surmise that I had a girl staying with me. But whatever they might think, they wouldn't intrude. Le Blanc would accept my decision and there would be no question of Anna being surprised. As for the unfortunate floor, it would have to wait.

Relieved, I said my goodbyes and set off for Val-en-Bretagne. Because of the difference in time zones it was too early to telephone the States. However, I hoped to catch my newspaper chum, and I needed to go to the bank and do one or two other things – such as parking the Jag.

150

I had forgotten it was market day. The town was buzzing with activity, littered with men, women, children, cars, carts, dogs, horses, poultry. Eventually I bribed an old woman to move a couple of crates of hens that were blocking a perfectly good parking place and edged in beside her stall.

I walked across to the hotel. The bar was full and I had to push my way through a throng of earnest drinkers. The air was thick with a mixture of garlic and Gauloises.

'Jean-Claude!'

'Jon!'

We beamed at each other and shook hands, long and hard, across the bar. Then he pushed up the flap for me and, gesturing to his assistant to take over, led the way through the bead curtains to the room in the rear. Here, because he was a dear friend whom I had known since I was a boy, I suffered myself to be kissed on both cheeks.

'Jon, this is marvellous. How are you, *mon vieux*?' He held me at arm's length and studied me. 'You look tired. Too much work or too many women?'

I laughed but I couldn't answer. The words choked in my throat. I yearned to tell him about Anna and Fel and the mess I had got myself into. But to confide in him would be pure self-indulgence. Resisting the temptation, I watched him produce a bottle of his best malt whisky, kept for special occasions, and pour us each a generous tot.

'*Santé!*' He grinned at me. 'I was thinking you might turn up, Jon.'

'You were? Why?'

I let the malt trickle around my mouth and seep warmly down my throat. I was at ease, more relaxed than I had been for days – and vulnerable.

'Your friends from Paris said they expected you – '

'What friends from Paris?'

'You mean they didn't find you?'

'Who?'

151

Jean-Claude had been about to refill our glasses but my interrogatives, exploding like sergeant-major's orders, startled him. He paused with the bottle in one hand.

'Something is wrong, Jon?'

'No, of course not,' I said, trying to ignore the sudden knotting of my insides. 'But I get enough visitors and entertaining in my job without being pursued when I'm on leave. Who were they? Do you remember what they called themselves?'

'*Bien sûr*. We don't run a huge luxury hotel. This is a small inn. To be exact, we have six bedrooms and when un-expected guests arrived last Tuesday night – '

'Tuesday?'

'Yes, Tuesday.'

Jean-Claude eyed me speculatively. He knew I was fraught but, if I didn't care to elucidate, he wasn't going to make a thing of it. Instead he attempted to forestall any possible questions.

'I didn't see their passports. They filled in their own *fiches*. They were a Monsieur and Madame Lesage, from Paris. Their Renault had Haut de Seine number plates. She was about thirty-five, a mousey blonde, but a determined woman. She did all the talking. I don't think I heard her husband say a word. He was older, middle to late forties, dark, beginning to bald, with strange – kind of dead eyes. Actually I wondered if he was a sick man.'

I swallowed hard. The knot in my guts had taken another twist. I knew no one, not even among my most distant acquaintances, called Lesage, and Jean-Claude had given a perfect description of Herr Werner Günther.

'What – what did they have to say about me, Jean-Claude?'

'They said you had suggested that while they were touring in Brittany they should come and visit you, but they'd lost the map you gave them. So they couldn't find your house and would I know how to get there.'

It was a plausible story. And it showed how efficient the communists were, how determined to recapture Anna. I tried to work out what must have happened.

When Anna fled at Oslo Airport Günther must have made an inspired guess that she would try to locate me. After all, it wasn't so improbable. I was one of the few delegates who lived in Oslo, and I had shown a fair amount of interest in her. He could have watched the flat, questioned the janitor, even phoned – or got a colleague to phone – with the excuse of a wrong number. And his guess had paid off.

Knowing Anna was with me, what would they have done? Günther had flown to Paris and collected a woman who clearly spoke fluent French. The two of them must have driven straight to Val-en-Bretagne ahead of me. But how did they know where I was going? Through the Embassy? I found it difficult to believe that they would have released my leave address to a casual enquirer. Through the janitor of my flat? Perhaps. In any case, they had arrived in Brittany before me, and had a clear idea of my whereabouts.

But what about the gadget on my car? What was that for? Presumably a kind of second string in case they had to cast about near Val-en-Bretagne to find my precise location.

'Jon!'

'Sorry, Jean-Claude. I was thinking.'

'That was evident,' he said dryly. 'But it is I who am sorry, Jon. I should never have told strangers where you lived.'

'It doesn't matter.' Grinning, I tried to reassure him. 'Admittedly they would have been unwelcome visitors at the moment, but you weren't to know that. It was my fault for having asked them.'

I drained my whisky. I told myself not to panic. Nevertheless, I was pushing back my chair, standing up. The telephone calls were important – I had to get in touch with Fel – but there was Anna alone in the house, and Günther . . .

'At any rate there's no harm done,' I said. 'I seem to have missed them.'

'Perhaps.' Jean-Claude shrugged. 'But they left only this morning. They might have tried once more, on their way, and if there were some sign that you were now in residence they might wait for you.'

'They wouldn't do that.' I spoke too positively.

'No? Probably not. They were in a hurry. They were angry with the German whose car was blocking theirs. I saw them arguing with him.'

'What German?'

'A Herr Kramer from Bonn. He arrived last night, also very late and unexpectedly, but there was no bed for him here. However, I felt sorry for him, even though he was a great big fellow and . . .'

I didn't listen any more. It must have been Horst. Knowing my probable destination and using the bug, he had found it simple to follow me across Europe. His only problem would have been the ferry to Denmark, and he could easily have taken the route through Sweden instead. In any case, the pursuers were assembled. Two had preceded me and one had followed. It was Anna they were after, and I might already be too late.

Chapter Three

THAT DAMNED OLD woman had wedged her crates of birds around the Jag. She had even put one on the roof; God knows what it was doing to the paintwork. Maybe she was hoping for yet another bribe, to persuade her to remove them. If that were so, she was going to be out of luck. Pushing and shoving them aside, I surprised her by the width of my French vocabulary and she was still shouting after me as I drove off.

I drove fast, wickedly fast, jabbing the horn in a sort of rhythm so that both man and beast were able to leap out of danger. I was lucky not to hit anything. Outside the town it was easier, but the lanes were narrow and winding, my car big. Twice I only just avoided an accident, first when rounding a corner I met a farm tractor head on, and secondly when some cows lumbered unexpectedly across my path on their way from one field to another. After that I was more circumspect.

Nevertheless, I must have broken all records, and I was drawing up in front of the house with a screech of tyres before I had given myself time to think. Everything looked quiet and peaceful. I don't know what I had expected but certainly not this ordinary scene. Half reassured I stumbled from the car. I was calling to Anna before I was in the hall.

'Anna! Where are you?'

She answered immediately. 'In here, Jon.'

There was a high note in her voice. It should have been a warning to me, but I was so relieved that Günther hadn't got

155

to her that I paid no attention. I burst into the living-room.

'Thank heavens you're all right. I was afraid – '

My words trailed away. She was sitting in my favourite big wing-chair with a hand on each of its arms. Her body was upright, her knees primly together. She looked stiff and uncomfortable. Suddenly an uncontrollable spasm shook her.

'Anna!' I took a step towards her.

'That's far enough, Mr Troy. Stop there, please.'

It was the woman who had spoken, the woman whom I had not previously met, the woman who called herself Madame Lesage. I wasn't mistaken. Jean-Claude had provided a pretty fair description and, if I had any doubts, the presence of Comrade Günther dispelled them. Both she and Günther were holding small but business-like guns.

'Sit down, Mr Troy,' Günther said. 'Where you are, on the carpet. Cross your legs and fold your arms, please.'

Warily I did as ordered. There wasn't much choice, though I didn't believe either of them would shoot. To kill me wasn't worth the danger it would involve, when all they wanted was to take Anna back with them.

'You've caused us a great deal of trouble, Mr Troy. Fräulein Mecklen is a very beautiful girl and it's understandable you should have been attracted to her, but that gave you no right to abduct her, no right whatsoever.'

Abduct her? I didn't say it aloud. I regarded Günther and then Anna with what I hoped was a blank expression. I wondered if he had invented the story in order to whitewash her defection – perhaps for his own sake since he had been in charge of their party – or if she had lied to protect herself. Günther returned my stare with a thin, nervous smile; he seemed oddly ill at ease. Anna didn't look at me. Her head was bent and her hair had dropped forward so that I couldn't see her face.

'I appreciate that the blame isn't entirely yours, Mr Troy,' Günther continued. 'Fräulein Mecklen ought never to have

156

allowed you to seduce her. It was a madness to come away with you to France and, of course, she'll pay for her stupidity, her wickedness, when she gets home. But what about you, Mr Troy? What are we going to do about you? I must admit you present us with a problem.'

He paused as if expecting some comment from me, but I ignored the veiled threat. It didn't bother me unduly. I was more concerned about what might happen when Anna was once again behind the Iron Curtain and her masters got the truth out of her, as they certainly would.

'Perhaps we should – er – remove Mr Troy while we consider the matter,' the woman suggested.

Günther nodded his agreement. 'That's a job for you, Horst.'

'My pleasure. There's a cellar to the house. He could wait there.'

I didn't attempt to turn round. I had been conscious for a while of someone to the rear of me and had guessed that it was Comrade Horst. He must have flattened himself behind the door as I stormed into the room or I would have heard him come in.

'Good,' Günther said. 'Clasp your hands on the top of your head, Mr Troy, and stand up slowly. Herr Horst will direct you. Just do what he says and don't try any tricks. We won't keep you incarcerated for long, so, as you English say, not to worry.'

I got to my feet obediently. Horst too had a gun. He gestured with it towards the hall and I went out of the room, along the passage and into the kitchen. Horst followed, keeping a careful distance from me in case I suddenly stabbed back at him. There was no hope of taking him by surprise.

In the kitchen I stopped in front of the cellar door. It was solid and close-fitting, kept shut by a heavy length of wood, hinged at one end, that dropped into slots each side. This could be my chance. I wondered if I might possibly wrench

157

free the wood and swing it around on Horst before he realized what was happening. I was sure he would hesitate to shoot me, but he was a big man and he moved fast.

I was still wondering when he said, 'One hand, Mr Troy. One hand only.' He must have read my thoughts. 'You don't need two to lift that bit of wood. Keep the other where I can see it.'

Reluctantly I obeyed. I took my time. Somehow the atmosphere had changed. Whereas Günther and the woman, tense though they were, had seemed to be acting out a kind of charade for my benefit, Horst implied a real menace.

'Mr Troy,' he said softly, 'do you remember that morning when you insulted me at the conference centre, turned me out of the kitchen where I had come to ask for the coffee?'

'I remember you being rude to Mrs Aasen, yes.'

'I wouldn't have permitted your insult then, except that your name was Troy. Now you are in a different position, and I can repay your insult as it should have been repaid before. No one, Mr Troy, no one behaves like that to Erich Horst and gets away with it.'

'Bully for you!' I said sarcastically.

I wanted to keep him talking, whatever rubbish it was. In his excitement he had moved nearer to me. I could almost feel his breath on my neck. He was being careless. I braced myself simultaneously to kick back at his shins and to swing round my arm so that my elbow landed in his gut. With any luck he would drop the gun, which would at least make the fight more even.

But again I had been too long thinking about it. I should have listened more understandingly to what he was saying. He wasn't just obeying Günther's orders. He was savouring a personal revenge.

I hadn't even begun to move when his fist crashed into my spine below the shoulder-blades. It was like being hit by a battering-ram. I was actually lifted up into the air before I started an uncontrolled dive down the cellar stairs, arms and legs flaying in a hopeless attempt to stop my fall. Some part of my body seemed to strike each separate step. Then I slithered across the cellar floor and drove my head straight into the side of a wine barrel.

I didn't lose consciousness but I was stunned. I lay on the ground. The ground was hard and everything was upside-down. My body was heavy. It wouldn't work properly. My mind wouldn't work properly either. It was because I was Troy that Horst hadn't been able to punish me? That didn't make sense. Someone had punished me – hurt me. I was battered and bruised. I wished the people who were talking so loudly would stop. My head throbbed and I yearned to sleep. They were talking in German. Anna. Poor Anna. Why couldn't they let her defect if that was what she wanted? And Fel? Maximillian Felard. Governor Felard. There could be a hell of a mess if Anna were forced to make accusations, if . . .

Suddenly I was fully aware. I knew where I was and how I had got there. But I didn't understand the voices that went on and on. It took me another minute to realize that I was listening to the East Germans. I was surprised how loudly they were talking. Though most of what they said was muffled I could catch the odd word, even the occasional phrase. Then the explanation came to me.

The cellar was large. It stretched the length of the house and, from where I lay, not far from the bottom of the steps, I was under the dining-room. But the conversation I could half-hear was taking place in the living-room. Why it sounded the way it did, why I could hear it at all, was because of the gaps in the boards of the sagging floor.

Apprehensively I got to my feet. For a moment or two I felt sick and giddy, but that passed though my head continued to throb. I took a few careful steps. Every bit of my body seemed to ache as if it had been used as a punching bag, and a sharp jab of pain in my shoulder suggested I had pulled a muscle. But I had been lucky. Nothing seemed broken.

Warning myself that if I was able to hear what was going on in the rooms above me it was possible that I might also be heard, I moved as quietly as I could. Small, barred windows, unwashed for months, let in a little light so that I could see what I was doing, but I had to take care. Apart from a meagre store of wine the cellar contained a lot of clutter, and I didn't want an unconsidered movement to dislodge a pile of logs or knock over a rusting bicycle.

The voices grew louder and more distinct as I passed beneath the hall and came to that part of the cellar directly below the living-room. They were angry, argumentative voices. My unwanted guests were quarrelling amongst themselves.

Hoping their differences might turn out to my advantage, I sat down on a convenient box to listen. The more I could find out about their plans, the more likely I was to be able to thwart them. I shut my eyes and tried to concentrate.

'. . . like to know why Troy returned so soon after he had left.'

'What does it matter, Horst?' That was Günther, barely containing his cold anger. 'He did return and he caught us, which means we're now dealing with a completely different situation.'

'It's a double problem, isn't it? What to do about Troy and what to do about Anna?' That was the woman speaking.

'Why don't we kill Troy?'

'Don't be a fool, Erich!'

'Kill Felard's son-in-law? You must be out of your mind.'

They must both have turned on Horst and I found myself grinning, though somewhat feebly. It was like listening to a radio play. The disembodied voices gave everything they said an air of unreality, though Horst's suggestion had been for real. He wouldn't hesitate to kill me if it suited his purpose.

160

Then suddenly I had something else to think about. It was Anna's voice: 'Be quiet, all of you. We are wasting time. Of course it's unfortunate that Troy caught you here. You had to contact me and find out what was happening. This place has no telephone, but you should have been more careful. However, there's no question of killing him. We shall leave him, tied up securely, but not too securely, so that he'll be able to free himself – not when it suits him but when it suits us, though naturally he won't appreciate that.'

Anna! It was Anna speaking. It couldn't be, but it was. 'Dear God!' I breathed the words as, fighting down my incredulity, I stared uncomprehendingly at the ceiling above me.

And Anna continued, shocking me into belief. Fräulein Anna Mecklen, the girl I had supposedly rescued – or failed to rescue – had taken command, was giving orders to her fellow-communists. I was appalled.

'. . . conscientious, so he'll contact Felard eventually and my dear papa will tell him he's already in touch with me. For Troy that will be the end of the matter.' Anna laughed. 'Perhaps I'll write him a nice letter thanking him for his help. After all, he might still be useful. He could substantiate a lot of my story if it were necessary.'

'It's the rest of your story that worries me. Having let you escape once, is it reasonable I should be such a moron as to let you run off a second time?' Günther snorted with disdain at the idea. 'Remember, I'm meant to be the clever one, not you, Anna, and even if we assume that once again you've easily outwitted me, what next? Here you are in France with nothing, no money, no clothes, no luggage. And you happen on a British newspaper which tells you that Governor Felard is at present staying with his old friend, Lord Linden, in Kent. No, no!' I could imagine him shaking his head. 'It stinks, Anna. Felard may be stupid, but he's not that stupid, and Robert Verson is nobody's fool.'

'But Verson doesn't know – '

'We don't know what he knows.' Günther interrupted brusquely; he seemed to speak to Anna on equal terms. 'Verson was spying on Felard at the conference – we caught him at it in that tunnel – and he may have discovered all sorts of things. Besides, it's my guess Felard will confide in him in the end.'

'I could say Eva helped me to escape, that she was sorry for me and – ' Anna began.

'Ah, good, yes!' It was the woman – Eva. 'I would have given her money and she could have bought herself a cheap suitcase.'

'And I suppose you would have told her that Felard was at the home of this Lord Linden? You saw it in a newspaper and just happened to mention it to her?' Günther's sarcasm was tangible.

'But it was in a paper,' Horst said. 'That's how – '

'I'm perfectly well aware of that. It was in the gossip column of a London daily, last Monday.' Günther's patience was ebbing fast. 'However, the chances of Anna ever having seen it are probably a million to one. We only know because our people monitor the English press, and at present any information on Felard has top priority.'

They went on arguing and I tried to digest what I had learnt. At least I knew now how they had found the house. Anna had told them we were going to Val-en-Bretagne – that was why she had been speaking German on the phone last Monday morning – and, when the bug on my car had failed them, Jean-Claude had provided instructions. How she must have laughed at the precautions I had taken. It made me sick to think of it. I had been completely taken in, and it was no consolation that Fel had been equally duped.

Because he most certainly had. If it hadn't been for the fire at the conference centre and Verson's high-handed behaviour afterwards, Fräulein Anna Mecklen of the GDR would already have begun the task of establishing herself close to him, if not actually in his household. But to what purpose? To obtain through Fel information that would be of value to her fellow-communists, to influence Fel subtly, to blackmail him by threatening his famous image, private and public?

There was no doubt she could have achieved all this – might still achieve it, if I didn't succeed in stopping her – but it was a long-term project. Fel would take every care. She wouldn't be able to press him too hard in the beginning. She might even have to spend two or three years in Britain or Canada before going to the States. And that didn't make sense.

Admittedly Fel was an important man. Because of his wealth and his family connections he would always carry a lot of clout, but his political power, which was what the communists would be interested in, rested mainly on his Governorship, and his second term of office was coming to an end. It was true he could stand again – a third term wasn't contrary to the State's laws – but it would be unusual, and a fourth term would be out of the question. What's more the obvious alternative, a Senate seat, wasn't open to him. Both the State's senators were young, able, popular and ambitious; they weren't going to step aside for Fel's benefit.

Which meant that by the time Anna's plans had matured, Fel might well be out of office, and what she had won so hardly of comparatively little value. Yet this conspiracy was no piddling thing. The East Germans had poured into it a great deal of effort, money and resources. The Russians, if not directly involved, were certainly interested; Boris Gronski had told me at the conference that he was an 'observer', and I was no longer in any doubt what he was observing. In any case, the GDR intelligence authorities wouldn't undertake a project of this scale without the acquiescence and co-operation of their Russian masters. Rumours of the plot, in a vague, distorted form, had even reached West German intelligence. The warning that Willi Schreiber had hesitated to give Fel had

163

to refer to Anna. He had said there were more ways to destroy a man than with a bullet.

While half my mind played with these questions, the other half was concentrated on the discussion taking place in the room above. In spite of Günther's scorn no one had come up with a better idea than that Anna should claim to have learnt of Fel's whereabouts from the press – not from the original London gossip column but from one of the more lurid French journals that could also be credited with a photograph of Fel.

'It's not good. I would have preferred something less coincidental,' Günther said. 'But it will have to do. We must be off. All right, Anna?'

'Yes. We can't waste any more time. Maybe one of us will think of a better plan on the way. Eric, go and fetch Troy.'

I was slow. I stood up quickly enough, but instantly sat down again as an excruciating pain sang through my spine and hammers banged on my skull. Horst was at the top of the cellar steps before I had reached the area under the hall.

'Troy, where are you?' When I didn't answer at once he repeated the question. 'Don't be a fool. I know you're down there. What are you doing?'

'Coming.' I didn't mind him being anxious, but I didn't want him to get curious.

'Hurry up! You're wanted.'

Light suddenly flooded the cellar – Horst had found the switch, which wasn't where one expected it to be but outside the door in the kitchen. Once he was able to see me limping towards him he relaxed, grinning unpleasantly. He waited while I climbed the stairs.

'Put your hands against the wall. Spread your feet.'

He patted me down with brisk efficiency and grunted when he found nothing. He was surprised I hadn't secreted something from the cellar to use as a weapon. He backed away from me cautiously.

'Right. Stand up. Go along to the living-room. But don't forget, I'll be just behind you, Troy. One false move and you'll regret it.'

I had no intention of making any sort of move. After what I had overheard I was quite content to allow myself to be tied up until Anna and the rest of them had gone. It was obviously the safest and the wisest thing to do.

'Come in, Mr Troy, and please sit over there,' Günther said.

Obediently I went across the room and sat down on the chair that Günther was indicating. It was like moving on to a stage set. I looked at him, at Eva, and lastly at Anna. Anna was crying quietly, hopelessly. Eva stood over her; she was giving a very good imitation of a wardress in a concentration camp. I nerved myself to play my part in the scene.

'What do you propose to do?' I asked.

'Nothing very drastic, Mr Troy. Fräulein Mecklen has already begun to see the foolishness of what she has done. She'll return with us – voluntarily. And you – well, I regret we shall have to leave you here, tied to that comfortable chair you're sitting in. After a bit of a struggle you'll get yourself free, but we'll be gone. It will be difficult to follow us. You'll find your car won't work and – yes?'

He paused, glanced at me enquiringly, waited for the interruption I was about to make. But I had managed to bite my tongue. My scathing comment on the time they had put sand in my petrol tank was stillborn. I had realized what a giveaway it would be.

'My advice to you, Mr Troy, is to be sensible. Don't try to cause any more trouble. Enjoy the rest of your vacation here in France and forget all about Fräulein Mecklen.'

'And if I choose not to take your advice?'

'Do as he says, please, Jon.' Anna raised a tear-stained face – she seemed able to cry at will – and looked at me beseechingly. 'It's best, believe me, for both of us. If you go to the authorities and attempt to make difficulties you'll achieve nothing – except perhaps to cause some inconvenience at a border. I – I must go home, *mein liebling*.'

'Anna, surely there's something – ' I began.

Eva interrupted me. 'It's getting late. We should be going, Werner.'

'Yes.' Günther nodded. 'Horst, go and find a piece of rope. There must be some around.' He gave me his thin-lipped smile. 'I'm sorry this is necessary, Mr Troy. I would like to take your word that you won't interfere again but I'm afraid it's impossible. I couldn't trust you.'

I glared at him. I wasn't quite sure how to behave. If I were too obstreperous they might decide to lay me out before they left me and, after Horst's attentions, I wasn't exactly in good shape. But if I were too supine they might get suspicious. I turned on Günther.

'Why don't you let Anna stay with me? You know that's what she wants – whatever you may have forced her to say. She can't matter so much to you. She's an ornithologist, not a nuclear physicist stuffed with vital information the West would love to have.'

I wound slowly to a halt. Günther had reached into the inside pocket of his jacket and had taken out a small, dark blue book with a coat of arms on the front. I knew at once what it was and cursed my stupidity. Günther held it up for me to see.

'The British passport you stole for Fräulein Mecklen, Mr Troy. It will, I think, ensure your good behaviour. Otherwise it will be sent to your ambassador with an explanatory note and will put an end to your promising career. I'm sure you don't want that to happen.'

Chapter Four

IT WOULDN'T BE true to say I had forgotten about the passport, but it had certainly slipped to the back of my mind. I hadn't given it a thought since Anna's duplicity had stopped me like a blockbuster. There had been too much else to consider. Now I faced the shattering fact that the only career I had ever wanted was about to come to an end.

I had stolen a British passport and processed it, not, as I had supposed, for an innocent girl – that was bad enough, though I had hoped to get away with it – but for a communist agent, and whatever Günther promised it would never be returned to me. I was wide open to blackmail. That left me no alternative. I would have to confess to my crime and offer my resignation – with luck I might avoid prosecution – because the one thing I was not going to do was start down the slippery slope from petty betrayal to high treason.

For the moment, however, no harm would be done if Günther accepted me as an incipient traitor. I managed a wan smile and shrugged my surrender. 'Okay. I'll do nothing, forget the whole episode. Come to think of it, there's not very much I could have done anyway.'

'That's sensible of you, Mr Troy.' Günther nodded approval. 'And as soon as we are all home I shall see to it myself that your passport – '

There was a thudding of heavy footsteps, the bang of a door flung back on its hinges, the crash of glass and china swept carelessly off a table. I winced, wondering what had been broken. Then Horst burst violently into the room and I had other things to occupy my mind.

'He knows! He knows!' Horst's voice shook with emotion.

'Knows what?' Günther snapped.

There was no doubt to whom Horst was referring. He was pointing a long thick finger straight at me. If I had been as innocent of guile as an angel I would have felt guilty. But perhaps I wouldn't have felt so afraid.

'Knows what?' Günther repeated.

'Everything! Everything we were saying when he was in the cellar. If you stand underneath this room you can hear every word, or almost every word. The carpet muffles the sound a little, but not much. I was searching for some rope to tie him up and I heard you clearly.'

Günther hadn't taken his eyes off me while Horst was speaking and I did my best to look blank and uncomprehending. I knew there was scant hope of deceiving him. But I had to try.

'I don't know what he's talking about, Herr Günther,' I whined, and to my disgust I sounded horribly natural. 'He shoved me down the cellar steps and by the time I'd recovered and gone into a corner to relieve myself, he was yelling for me to come up again.'

'I wonder . . .' Günther's stare seemed to bore into me. 'Have I underrated you, Mr Troy? We'll have to find out, won't we?' With an apparently careless gesture he directed his gun at my crutch. 'Eva, go down to the cellar, please, and listen. Mr Troy and I are going to have an interesting conversation. You start, Mr Troy.'

'I – I don't understand. You make it sound as if we were playing some sort of game.'

'Perhaps that's what you thought we were doing. You English think of most things in terms of sport. And you pride yourselves on being good losers, don't you? Are you a good loser, Mr Troy? I suspect that very soon we shall discover.'

Fear is supposed to sharpen one's mind but it wasn't having that effect on me. In a handful of minutes Günther would know that Horst hadn't exaggerated, that I had heard them give themselves away. Probably he knew already but was taking the opportunity to rethink the situation. So far Anna had given no sign. She appeared to be lost in misery. Günther could be waiting for her, rather than for Eva. He could afford to wait. There was nothing I could do.

'Talk, Mr Troy! Talk.'

'For God's sake, what about?' I allowed myself a spurt of anger. 'You'll be asking me to sing next. What would you like? My national anthem?'

Günther shook his head. 'No, Mr Troy. That won't be necessary.'

Eva had been quick. She appeared now without any show of haste or emotion such as Horst had displayed. Indeed she seemed more occupied with a snag in her tights than with anything else. And when she spoke she was calm, indifferent. She might have been making some comment on the weather.

'Erich was right. From below you can hear everything that is said in this room. Troy will have to die.'

'Die! You mean you're going to kill me? But that's absurd.' I mimed a stunned disbelief. 'Herr Günther, I appeal to you. You're a reasonable man. You can't really intend to kill me.'

'Why not, Mr Troy?'

'But – but why should you? You'd be taking an awful risk, and for what? I could hear your voices when I was in the cellar, I admit, but not what you were saying, and I know nothing about whatever it is that's so important to you.'

'He's lying.' Horst put an end to my babbling.

'I'm inclined to agree with you, Horst,' Günther said slowly. 'But it's irrelevant. We could never be quite sure.

169

And we can't afford to be wrong. No. It's a pity.' He sighed. 'I regret it – not just because of you, Mr Troy, but because your death will present us with more problems. However, I'm afraid it's inevitable.'

'But it must appear accidental.'

I drew a long, shuddering breath. Anna had tossed back her glorious hair and was regarding me as if I were a total stranger. I knew she wouldn't show me any mercy.

'All right,' I said angrily. 'I did hear what you were talking about – some of it. I know Anna isn't Fel's daughter and you're planning to set him up in some way, but why should I care? God knows I've no reason to love my ex-father-in-law. Besides, as long as you've got that bloody passport I can't do a thing.'

'Don't be stupid, Troy.'

Anna stood up. She flexed her arms and loosened her shoulder muscles. I half expected her to start running on the spot like an athlete before the big event. She seemed to slough off her despondency, her resignation, her fear, and become a different woman, full of power and purpose; suddenly she reminded me forcibly of Fel.

'The temptation to whisper a warning to the great Felard would be too strong for you,' Anna said decisively. 'However, we'll make your death as painless as we can. After all, you and I are related by marriage, Troy. Because you were wrong. Maximillian Felard is my father. That's why what I'm going to do to him will give me so much pleasure.'

'What are you going to do?' At that precise moment I didn't give a damn, but the question was forced out of me.

'Well, that depends on a lot of things. Of course duty has priority, but on this occasion duty and personal revenge happen to be one.' Suddenly her face contorted with hatred. She was ugly. It was a startling transformation. 'Felard walked out on my mother. She died in poverty a few years later. He betrayed her, and me. But what did he care? He

170

had no love for us, alive or dead. Now I'm going to make him betray what he does love.'

'Anna,' Günther said softly.

'Yes, Werner. Yes.' She was breathing hard. 'I know. First we must decide how to deal with Troy.'

It didn't take them long to reach a decision. After the shortest of whispered conferences they went into action. While Eva covered me with a gun Horst tied my hands behind me. Then he knocked me back into the chair with a sickening blow to my lower abdomen. More personal revenge.

The room spun around me. Eva rebuked Horst, told him to be more careful. Careful? There were footsteps upstairs and sounds from below, from the cellar. I tried to work out what they meant but my head was splitting.

Aware that Horst had pulled off my shoes and socks, I suddenly revolted. He had started to work on my trousers. With all the strength I could muster I kicked out at him, and gasped as the gun ground into the side of my neck.

'Mr Troy, I don't want to shoot you but if necessary I will. Have no doubt of it. As Herr Günther implied new situations make new problems but we can always adapt our plans. We're very versatile.'

Eva spoke calmly. She was unmoved by the incident. And I had achieved nothing, except some personal satisfaction. Horst, his face screwed up with pain, was hugging himself between the legs.

'Come, Erich,' Eva said. 'We must be quick. And you, Mr Troy, co-operate. It'll be better for you if you do.'

Gritting his teeth Horst approached me again. As if by chance he trod heavily on my right foot, and I nearly bit through my lower lip to stop myself from crying out. I let him pull off my trousers. I knew what was coming next. He put his hand into the top of my underpants and wrenched them down. Half naked, I felt horribly vulnerable.

171

'Stand up, Troy. Turn around – and behave yourself, or God help you.'

'God help me? Surely as a good Red you don't believe in God, do you, Horst?'

I don't know why I deliberately riled him. Perhaps it was to keep my mind off the fact that I might not have much longer to live. Perhaps it was to put up a front and so give myself some spurious courage. At any rate I couldn't resist the temptation.

This time Horst didn't react. Quickly and deftly he untied my hands, slipping off my watch at the same time, and tied up my ankles. I didn't try anything.

'Your jacket.' He jerked it back off my shoulders and pulled it over my arms. 'Your shirt.'

I was slow with the shirt. There were buttons to be undone, cuff-links to be removed. I didn't hurry. It wasn't that I was modest or that I minded displaying myself. Eva must have seen a full-frontal nude before now. But somehow I felt what courage I had left – false or otherwise – oozing away with each garment I removed. I took off my shirt with extreme reluctance.

'Throw your cuff-links behind you, Mr Troy,' Eva said. 'And stand still!'

She snapped her last order, though I can't imagine what she thought I might do. Admittedly Horst would be bending down behind me to pick up the links; but I was naked, my ankles hobbled and, worst of all, my mind wasn't functioning as it should. If there had been an opportunity I had missed it.

'Turn!'

I turned, in two hops. Anna was coming through the door. She carried my robe, a pair of pyjamas and some slippers. Her eyes flicked me up and down and against my will I felt myself stir. Horst sniggered.

'Get him dressed,' Anna said. 'Quickly.'

This time I put up no resistance, not even of a passive

kind. I hurried into my pyjamas and robe. Ludicrously my spirits rose. And they didn't tie me up again. Though I guessed this was only because they didn't want to leave any marks on my body it was encouraging.

At a gesture from Eva I sat down again. Anna had moved behind me. I couldn't see what she was doing but I could hear. She was pouring a drink. Then she came around the chair and held out a tumbler three-quarters full of whisky. She had been careful to wrap the glass in a handkerchief so as to avoid fingerprints.

'Take it, Troy.' I hesitated and she added, 'It's not poisoned. We're going to make you drunk, *mein liebling*, give you a few pills and, as soon as you're asleep, push you down the cellar stairs. When you wake up we'll be gone and you'll be in your nice bourgeois heaven. What more can you ask?'

'What indeed, Anna?'

It was an automatic reply. I had started to flog an unresponsive brain. My chances of coming out of this alive were low. There were four of them to my one, and in any physical set-to I hadn't a hope. But I knew what they were planning to do with me. I could still outwit them, if I were clever enough.

'Drink it. Fast, Jon.'

I drank it as slowly as I dared, while she stood over me. It made no difference. I had had two glasses of wine with the Le Blancs at the farm and two whiskies with Jean-Claude in Val-en-Bretagne. Anna's potion, though I managed to spill a little, almost knocked me out. Not quite. I had eaten a large breakfast – Madame Le Blanc had stocked the refrigerator with eggs and bacon – and I had eaten it late. Perhaps that was what saved me. Perhaps it was sheer bloody-mindedness. At any rate I managed to cling to reality.

But I was like a man hanging by his finger tips above an abyss, and slipping, millimetre by millimetre. Any second I would plunge into nothingness. Meanwhile the room revolved around me. Faces came and went, loomed large over me, shrank into dots. There seemed to be a lot of activity. They were getting ready to clear out. Someone – Anna – fixed my hand around another glass of whisky.

'Drink it. Go on. Drink.'

I drank. Oddly enough, though I would never have passed a breathalyser test, I felt more sober. And I succeeded in spilling half the liquid.

'You're not going to get away with this,' I said. My voice was slurred and I had difficulty articulating my words. 'You'll see. Fel's no fool. He'll want to know what you did with me. How are you going to explain why you left me, Anna? Eh? How you going to explain that?'

'Easy, *mein liebling*. Easy. I'll say you tried to rape me, so I had to run away. I'll say Eva picked me up on the road and took me to Paris and – '

Rape? No! Not rape! Not again! I'd taken it once, because of Carol. Because she'd never questioned the bloody lie, because she'd been glad to be rid of me. But not a second time. No. I'd fight. This time I'd fight.

I was on my feet. I struck out at yet another glass of whisky that Anna was offering me and sent it flying. The third. Or was it the fourth? Spraying liquor across the carpet it hit the edge of a table and broke. Anna cried out. Someone was shouting obscenities. As I staggered across the room I realized it was me. My legs gave way and I collapsed on the floor. Horst and Günther helped me back to the chair.

'He's had enough alcohol,' Günther said. 'Give him the pills and let's get on.'

There were five of them, five yellow and white capsules containing multi-coloured granules. I had no idea what they were. I never use sleeping-pills myself. But I knew they could mean the end of me and I had to do something about them. I didn't know what.

Anna brought me the soda-water. Eva pushed the first

capsule into my mouth. I swallowed it and drank all the soda-water, which annoyed them. They brought more soda-water. I swallowed the second capsule but when they gave me the third I simultaneously spewed it out of my mouth and knocked away the glass. While they searched for the capsule I managed to thrust it deep down into the cleavage of the chair cushions.

My next effort wasn't so successful. I pretended to choke and purposely lost the damned thing down the front of my pyjamas, but Anna had seen. Holding my nose and forcing open my mouth she enabled Eva to drop the last two capsules down my throat. I swallowed them quickly. Time was now all important to me.

I offered no more resistance. Willingly – trying not to show my eagerness – I allowed myself to be half dragged, half supported across the living-room, down the hall, into the kitchen. The door to the cellar was wide open and the light was on. I prayed that they would hurry, that I wouldn't be too late. A lot would depend on how I landed at the bottom of the stairs. If it was like the last . . .

There wasn't room for the three of us in the doorway. Günther stepped back and Horst shifted his grip on my arm so as to take more of my weight. Now, my brain screamed. Now, before his fist slams into that same spot between the shoulder-blades and you black out with the pain. His hold on me was loose. Hampered by my sagging body he was taking a moment to get himself into position. Now! But it had to look like an accident.

Heaving a great drunken sigh I pulled myself free. For a wild moment I teetered on the top stair. Then I let myself crash down to the bottom. Horst gave a shout. I think I must have damn near taken him with me, which would have been a mistake; he could have knocked all the breath out of me. As it was, the fall was no joy.

In some ways it was worse than last time because my body

was already a mass of bruises. But it wasn't so violent and, though I landed in practically the same place, I managed to cover my head with my arms and minimize the impact with the barrel. Nevertheless, my strength had gone.

I lay, wishing the two of them would go away and leave me alone. I was very tired. I wanted to sleep. It was quite comfortable on the cellar floor and I could feel myself drifting off. But they weren't going away. They were coming down the stairs. One of them kicked me in the ribs. I was on my front and couldn't see which, but I was sure it was Horst. I blessed him. He had forced me awake again.

'He's still alive.' Another dig in the ribs and I had to grunt.

'It doesn't matter. Better he dies in his sleep.' That was Günther. He lifted my head by a handful of hair and let it drop. 'Come on. We've no more time to waste.'

Horst sniggered. 'He doesn't look much like raping anyone at the moment, does he?'

Günther didn't answer. Anna was calling and he started up the stairs. I waited for Horst's final blow, trying not to tense myself. Instead he reached down, pulled up my head as Günther had done and spat in my face. Then he was pounding after his comrade. The door shut. The lights went off, and went on again.

I couldn't wait any longer. I was thrusting two fingers down my throat, tickling the roots of my tongue. I gagged but I wasn't sick. I thought of the most disgusting things to eat I could imagine, from putrid flesh to human excrement. My stomach muscles went into spasm. But my hand was slipping from my mouth, my mind was drifting aimlessly, my body was something apart.

When it came – a thin stream of greenish bile – I didn't realize at first that it came from me. I lay in it. I was on the borderland of sleeping and waking. I didn't want to be disturbed. But the smell reached me and by some trick of memory I was back in that police van on that fatal night I met

176

Darlene Smith. There was the same stench, a mixture of whisky and vomit, and the same incomprehension as to what was happening.

Rape. You raped her. Raped her. Raped her. Verson's voice. Horst's voice. Fel's. Carol's.

With a tremendous effort I pushed two unwilling fingers back down my throat. Once more my stomach contracted. Nausea overwhelmed me. And now, having begun, it seemed I couldn't stop. Again and again I vomited until at last, completely spent, I rolled away from my own filth. I let my eyelids droop. I let waves of sleep flow over me. There was nothing more I could do. If – if I ever woke up, everything would be different.

I woke. Slowly I rose through seas of cotton wool. I lay on the surface. It was hard, uncomfortable. Once or twice I began to sink. I would have been happy to sink, but somehow it wasn't possible. They say that if you can swim you can't drown without a struggle. I struggled.

Eventually, I triumphed. I was fully awake, though the bright light worried my eyes. There was something odd about the light. The black squares, the windows, gave me the clue. Outside it was night. It was only the two naked electric bulbs that made the cellar so like day. Time had passed.

By now they must have gone, Günther, Horst, Eva – and Anna, long gone. And I was alive! In my excitement I got to my knees and tried to stand. My legs wouldn't work properly. It wasn't altogether their fault. I soon discovered that when I moved my head, unless it was very slowly, the floor tilted and the whole cellar swung round and round.

'Gently,' I admonished myself. 'Gently does it.'

The words startled me. They were loud and slurred and cheerful. They weren't mine, any more than these limbs were mine. It took me a full minute to realize that the drink and the drugs had left me with a monumental hangover. I began to laugh.

I didn't laugh long. It hurt too much. After some delicate probing I decided that at least one of my ribs was cracked. With equal care I examined the rest of my body. It was covered with bruises and abrasions. There was matted blood in my hair. I had pulled a muscle in my shoulder and had probably sprained a wrist. But, incredibly, nothing was broken.

And I was alive. For a while I sat and savoured the fact. My mind was turning over slowly and heavily. I knew I had a lot to do but it was all so difficult. My thoughts kept sliding off at a tangent. I had to clean myself up. I needed help. Jean-Claude. Long way to Val-en-Bretagne. I couldn't drive in my present state. Perhaps I could make it to the farm, if Horst hadn't sabotaged the Jag again. But that was a different plan, when I wasn't meant to die. I must get to Fel. They'd told me where he was. Lord Linden. I could telephone. Supposing Fel didn't believe me. He hadn't believed me about Darlene Smith. To hell with him. I'd face that when I came to it.

First things first. I disciplined my thoughts. The first thing was to get myself out of the cellar. I concentrated on that. I couldn't stand so I crawled. It took me some time to reach the bottom of the stairs. My robe was a nuisance. It was comparatively short but it got in my way and I determined to get rid of it. In my semi-drunken state this wasn't easy. To my surprise I flaked out again.

I came to with my head pillowed on the bottom step, the robe in a tangled, torn heap beside me. I started to climb. It was a long, painful process. I remember being thankful for the light and then thinking that of course they had had to leave it on. Presumably I was meant to have heard a noise in the night and, going to investigate in a half drunk, half doped condition, had fallen down the stairs and killed myself. But the plan hadn't worked because I had sicked up most of the drugs they had given me. And here I was, alive and if not well at least at the top of the cellar stairs.

Gingerly I stood up. I pushed open the door into the kitchen. The door didn't open. I pushed again, without result. Holding on to the handle I threw my weight against the door but it still didn't budge and suddenly, hopelessly, wildly, not caring how much I hurt my torn shoulder, I flung myself at it, again and again. I was sobbing with frustration but it did no good.

Chapter Five

I GOT CONTROL of myself fairly quickly. I was ashamed of my outburst and, to save face, blamed it on the dope I had taken. I started to use my brain again.

The door offered no hope. It was firmly shut. The hinged length of wood must somehow have dropped into place. The hinge was a little loose and maybe the final bang of the front door had done it. Or more likely Horst, stupid to the last, had done it himself as a kind of double insurance, without the others knowing. In any case I was imprisoned.

Permanently? Surely not. There had to be some way of getting out of the cellar. The windows were the best bet. To inspect them I went down the stairs on my bottom. It was the safest means. I couldn't trust myself to walk. I felt weak and sick and dizzy, but determined.

The windows were very small, high up and nailed shut. I would never be able to squeeze myself through. Fighting down my disappointment I stood on tip-toe and peered out. It was impossible to see the sky but I got the impression that the darkness was less opaque than it had been. I caught myself looking at my wrist but they had taken my watch and I had no idea what the time was. I wished that day would come.

Not that it was likely to do me much good. No one ever came to the house. The rare letter I received, such as a bill for the electricity or the local taxes, would be delivered to the farm. Butter, milk and cream I collected myself, but there was plenty in the refrigerator. Madame Le Blanc had stocked it well. She wouldn't miss me if I didn't turn up for a week or more and, since I had told Le Blanc yesterday that the sagging floor in the living-room would have to wait, he wouldn't be around either. That left a few friends in Val-en-Bretagne, but they were French and none would drop in uninvited, not even Jean-Claude. I smiled sourly as I remembered explaining the advantages of all this to Anna.

Still, miracles did happen. I had to believe that. Le Blanc or Jean-Claude or someone might come looking for me – though not in the middle of the night. And I was very tired. I yearned to rest. By morning the worst of my Olympian hangover should have worn off, the sleep would surely have done me good and generally I might be better equipped to deal with my unpleasant situation.

At least there was no fear that I wouldn't wake up again. On the contrary, the difficulty now was to get to sleep. I had so many aches and pains. The floor was hard. I was cold. I thought longingly of a comfortable bed, an electric blanket . . .

I must have triggered some memory that linked up with another, and another, until suddenly I recalled the curtains. My mother had always insisted that in the spring the winter curtains should be taken down, cleaned, packed away and replaced by the summer curtains. In the autumn the reverse took place. My father had long given up the practice in England, but not so Madame Le Blanc. Somewhere in the cellar there must be a box of winter curtains.

In my feeble state it took me what seemed like an age to locate the right box but, when I did, it was a major triumph. The curtains were of velvet, long, heavy and lined. I made myself a sort of sleeping-bag out of them with a pillow for my head, wrapped myself in a spare and got in. As a bed it wasn't luxurious but it was warm and after some rearrangement to protect my face from the brightness of the electric bulbs I settled down. Almost at once I was asleep.

I woke lazily, worried by the smell until I managed to place it. It was camphor. The curtains stank of it, and so did I. I hadn't noticed it before, which shows how far gone I had been in the night. I was feeling much better now.

It was morning. I could tell that from the light coming through the windows and the song of the birds in the garden outside. I got up slowly. My wrist was swollen. My ribs hurt if I breathed too deeply. My whole body was stiff. But I was no longer drunk or doped. When I stood the cellar didn't revolve. Ceiling, walls and floor behaved as they should. I could actually walk upright. I didn't have to crawl. It was extraordinary how much pleasure that simple fact gave me.

My most immediate need was for something to drink. My stomach was still queasy and the idea of food revolted me, but I could have done with a gallon of black coffee. It was useless to think of it. I knew I would have to settle for wine which was the only thing available, and even that I would have to ration. There was sugar in wine and sugar was nourishment. I wondered how long one could stay alive on a bottle of wine. A week? Ten days? I might survive down here for months. And I would be missed before then. The Office would make enquiries. The FCO didn't like its people to disappear; it was very suspicious. Someone would come and rescue me.

Reassured by this thought, I set off to count the number of bottles in the racks and I found half a dozen tonic water, which was an unexpected bonus. It took me minutes to get the cap off one, but when I did I drank the whole bottle – as a treat.

I wasn't as healthy as I had imagined. Without warning, tiredness sandbagged me. I had to go and rest. I didn't intend to sleep but my eyelids were heavy, my limbs light, and gently I floated into space.

This happened intermittently throughout the long day. In the intervals I did some general housekeeping and explored the cellar, every stick and stone, every box, bottle, bit of rusting wire. I found nothing useful, except for some discarded china and a heap of old newspapers. I now had a cup from which to drink my wine and I was able to remake my bed with a base of cardboard and a mattress of paper. I also spent a lot of time staring out of the window.

When at last it was dark outside and I permitted myself to go to bed, I had to make an effort not to think of tomorrow and the day after and the day after that. I was afraid that I might soon regret ever having woken up in the cellar.

It wasn't the best of nights. I slept fitfully, again and again frightening myself awake with a series of nightmares. When dawn came with its bird song and sunshine filtering through the windows, I was tempted to lie in. Pride prevented me. I knew it would be a bad precedent. Steeling myself, I attended to my toilet, made my bed, inspected the weather and had breakfast. Breakfast was half a bottle of tonic water.

Even making every action last as long as possible I can't have taken more than twenty minutes over the whole thing, but I did have something in reserve. During the night I had realized that if I were to survive any length of time in these conditions I had to provide myself with physical and mental exercise, and in the sleepless hours I had worked out a regimen for myself. I proposed to begin it now.

With a sprained wrist, a pulled shoulder muscle, one or two cracked ribs and a split head, I didn't intend to do handstands or turn somersaults. I intended to be very careful. I started with a few gentle exercises and followed these by running on the spot. It wasn't a great success. I felt worse afterwards than before.

My idea for mental exercise proved a much better proposition. It consisted of taking a newspaper – I chose a *Figaro* for today's effort – and tearing out words, phrases, whole sentences, which I could arrange on a piece of cardboard to form a message. I hoped there would be no need for it but, if I were going to die in the cellar, I wanted to leave some warning about Anna, I wanted to tell Carol and Paul that I loved them, I wanted the police to know I had been murdered and by whom. I thought of more and more things I had to say.

It was a splendid game. It needed care and concentration, which meant it was distracting and enabled me to forget my ills, at least for a while. Best of all, it gave me something to do. It was time-consuming.

At intervals I stood up and, at a safe distance so as not to cause a draught and disturb my pieces of paper, did some exercises. When I judged it might be about noon I finished the tonic water, broke the neck of another bottle of wine and poured myself a cup. I drank it slowly. This was my lunch. Then, feeling mildly pleased with my morning's achievements, I once again settled down to the game.

The doorbell rang.

I paid no attention. I was absorbed with what I was doing. I had just found the word *Félicitation*, with a capital F. The accent was unimportant. I now had 'Fel'. The 'ard' would be easy.

The doorbell rang, and in my mind there was a residual memory that it had rung before.

Suddenly aware, I leapt up, scattering bits of newspaper, knocking aside my cardboard tray, displacing pathetic words which moments ago had given me such pleasure. On my feet, I hesitated. All the windows down here faced to the rear of the house. Ignoring them, I ran to the part of the cellar that was beneath the front door. I had seized a broomstick on my way. I banged as high up on the wall as I could reach, shouting and shouting.

Then I stopped and listened. I could hear the thudding of my heart. Otherwise there was silence – except for a strange scratching sound, a thud, steady tapping. Someone had inserted a key in the lock, opened the front door and walked into the hall. I didn't waste any more time. I made for the stairs and practically threw myself up them.

'Madame Le Blanc! C'est moi, Monsieur Troy! Ouvrez la porte, je vous en prie. Ouvrez la porte!'

There was no answer. But it had to be Madame Le Blanc. The footsteps had been a woman's and only the Le Blancs had a key.

I tried again. *'Madame!'* Her presence on the other side of the door was all but tangible. *'Madame! C'est –* '

'Jon! Jon, is that you?'

I froze. It wasn't Madame Le Blanc. Whoever it was had spoken in English and with the soft drawl that belonged way south of the Mason-Dixon line. Carol? Questions tumbled over themselves. How could it be Carol?

Keeping my voice level and sensible, I said, 'Yes. It's me – Jonathan Troy.'

I heard her fumbling with the piece of wood, then the door opened, and I staggered into the kitchen. My relief at being free dulled my amazement that it should have been Carol who had freed me. I stared at her disbelievingly.

It was years since I had seen my ex-wife and she had changed. She was still beautiful, a tall girl, with wide grey eyes and a cap of shining blonde hair – more beautiful than I remembered. But there were lines around her mouth that hadn't been there before. She looked tired, withdrawn, and the expensive clothes, the meticulous grooming, the aura of luxury that had always been an essential part of her, seemed now to be a carapace for her to hide behind.

'I'd forgotten you had a key to this house,' I said stupidly.

'I – I should have sent it back to you.'

185

'I'm glad you didn't.'

The bathos of this conversation hit us both at the same time. We smiled at each other. And suddenly it was all too much for me. I wasn't going to die, trapped like an animal under ground. I was safe. Water to drink, water to wash in. A bath, clean clothes, food. Everything was mine for the taking. I could go into the garden, see the sky. And Carol was here with me, Carol whom I loved more than anyone in the world, Carol . . .

I was unaware that I had spoken her name aloud. I stumbled across to a chair, pillowed my head on the kitchen table and wept.

'Jon. Jon.' She held me close.

'Sorry,' I pushed her gently away. 'Better not touch me. I'm filthy dirty. I've been down there since – since Friday – and it's not exactly Claridges.'

'Friday? But, how – ? What happened, Jon?'

I didn't want to lie to her but I couldn't tell her the truth either. It was too complicated and there was the problem of Fel and Anna. I shook my head in frustration, caught my breath and gave a shuddering sob of pain.

Carol was quick. 'It doesn't matter. Not now. You're hurt. Come on, Jon, I'll take you upstairs and then go and get a doctor. Do you know one in Val-en-Bretagne?'

'I don't want a doctor. I'll be all right when I've washed and had something to eat.' I rubbed my hand over my chin. I badly needed a shave. 'Will you help? I'm sorry to ask but – '

'Don't be silly. Just – just tell me what you'd like.'

'Let's start with a glass of water, then.'

'Okay. Coming right up.'

The emotional moment was over. Carol dressed the cut in my head, ran my bath, helped me into it. She was considerate, efficient, and as unloving as a nurse taking a practical examination.

I concentrated on what had to be done. Nothing came

easy. Washing, shaving, even cleaning my teeth seemed to require two hands, and Carol was right, I did need a doctor. My left wrist was very swollen and my whole arm ached, up to my shoulder and across my back. And the sight of my face in the mirror shocked me. My eyes were sunk deep in my head, their surrounds bruised. My skin was jaundice-coloured. I looked like hell!

Dressing was a long, laborious business. Carol had gone downstairs and I was damned if I was going to call to her. I had seen the look of disgust she had given the rumpled bed, the almost empty bottle of whisky, the dirty glass. She had interpreted them exactly as the East Germans had intended, as anyone would interpret them, but that didn't make me feel any less bitter. I had always expected more of Carol than of other people.

Depressed, I went downstairs. I knew I should be thankful to be alive and out of that bloody cellar, but at the moment I could only think of the problems ahead. Carol, in one of Madame Le Blanc's aprons, was sweeping the kitchen floor. She had made a heap of glass and china – the remains of my breakfast with Anna, her half-sister. Suddenly, inexplicably, I was glad that there was little if any resemblance between the two girls.

'You seem to have had an accident, Jon.'

'Yes.' I thought of Comrade Horst. 'But don't bother about it. How's the coffee doing?'

'It's ready. Scrambled eggs, tomatoes, toast?'

'That would be fine.'

I sat back, sipped my coffee, watched Carol cook. Inevitably I recalled the first time I had brought her here, how happy we had been, exquisitely, almost painfully happy, and Paul had been conceived. Even then, before my leave was over, Fel was demanding her return. Wife gave way to dutiful daughter. The halcyon days ended. It had never been quite the same again.

'Carol, there are some questions I need to ask.'

'Such as why I've paid you this surprise visit?'

'We could start with that, yes.' My voice was harsh.

'Fel sent me. He called your ambassador in Oslo to find out where you were and Sir William's secretary, Jane – Jane someone – '

'Hamlin.'

'Jane Hamlin said you had gone to your house in Brittany. No phone, of course, so Dad asked me to go and fetch you.'

'Go and fetch me?' How typical of Fel, I thought. It didn't matter what you were doing; if he wanted you, you came.

'Yes, I've no idea what it's about, but it's urgent. He must talk with you.'

'He's staying with Lord Linden?'

Carol was surprised. She nodded. 'I've a private jet waiting at Dinard airport. If we hurried we could be with Dad tonight. But – ' She hesitated. 'You're not really in a fit state to travel, are you, Jon? We'll have to wait until tomorrow at least.'

I made no immediate response. If Fel wanted me with such urgency it could only mean that Anna was already in touch with him. But what had she told him? If she had produced her rape story, why should he want me?

'What about Bob Verson, Carol?'

'What about him? He's with Dad – at Lord Linden's. They went there from Oslo.'

'And you joined them?'

'Yes. Bob asked me to come. He was worried.' She stopped, flushed and added, 'Stupid of him, actually. When I got there, Dad was fine. I needn't have flown over after all.'

'But you stayed?'

'Yes. I stayed.' Her hand shook as she refilled my empty coffee cup. 'Why not? What are you suggesting, Jon?'

I hadn't the faintest idea what I was suggesting. If she had stayed because of Verson it was none of my business. If she had stayed because of Fel who, I was beginning to suspect, had been suffering from more than smoke inhalation, again it wasn't my business. But why should my question have embarrassed her so much?

I said: 'Just one more thing I'd like to know, Carol, then we'll be off. Don't worry about me. I'll survive the journey. I want to see Fel as much as he seems to want to see me. But first, tell me. Is Bob Verson aware that you've been sent to – er – "fetch" me?'

'No. He isn't. Dad said it was a private matter. I wasn't to mention it to Bob or – or anyone. And for God's sake don't ask me why, because I haven't a clue. Dad just said, "Bring him. I need him. If he refuses to come – "'

'Yes,' I said and felt my guts contract. 'Go on, Carol. If I refused, what were you to do?'

'I – I was to remind you of Darlene,' she said glacially.

Chapter Six

CAROL DROVE. I sat beside her, trying not to wince too often. She had made a sling for my arm out of a scarf and that helped, but whenever she braked sharply, pain flared from the tips of my fingers to my shoulder and back again. Realizing this, she was driving as carefully as she could, but the Renault she had rented at the airport was strange to her and she didn't know the road. Each time I winced she said, 'Sorry.' We were being very polite to each other.

Since the mention of Darlene's name the temperature had dropped about five degrees. I had finished my coffee quickly and refused more food. We left the house soon afterwards.

I would have liked to take the Jag, but obviously I couldn't drive and we couldn't leave the Renault. I asked Carol to start my car, to make sure it was all right. And she did, and it was; Comrade Horst hadn't played any tricks.

We went first to the farm. I was lucky enough to catch Le Blanc coming out of the barn. I told him I had accidentally shut myself in the cellar and had been there for a couple of days and would he please clear up the mess himself and not let his wife do it. He was a practical man. He would assume I had been drunk but he would do as I asked, and he wouldn't gossip.

I settled down to nursing my arm and giving Carol directions until we were through Val-en-Bretagne and on the Route Nationale. When there was no longer a need to navigate we lapsed into silence. There were so many things I wanted to ask her, but somehow I didn't know where to begin. And the silence grew into an ache.

It was Carol who made the breakthrough. 'Why didn't you marry her?' she asked conversationally.

'Marry who?' I had been thinking of Anna – though most certainly not in terms of marriage – and I must have sounded vague.

'Your girl-friend. Darlene.'

'What?' I swallowed hard. Carol had been about to overtake a car with a trailer and at the last moment had decided not to. 'Are you mad? Darlene wasn't a girl-friend of mine. I'd never met her before that night. As for marrying her – '

'Sorry, Jon. My mistake. But when you wrote to tell me you were leaving me, you mentioned a girl-friend in Washington. I – I thought that must be Darlene.'

I turned in my seat and stared at her. She didn't look at me. She kept her eyes on the road. Her face, I saw, was screwed up as if she were angry or having to make a great effort not to cry, and she was gripping the steering wheel so hard that her knuckles were like ivory. Suddenly the words came tumbling out of her.

'How could you do it, Jon? How could you walk out on me and Paul, as if we were nothing to you? Oh, I know I said everything was over between us, but you must have known I didn't mean it. When they're angry people say all sorts of things they don't mean. And this girl in Washington – if she'd been really important to you, you'd have married her. Why didn't you marry her, Jon?'

'Because – because she didn't exist,' I said slowly.

I was still staring at Carol, my mind sorting the implications of what she had been saying, trying to make sense of them, trying to fit them into a pattern, trying to understand. It wasn't easy to think. She had just turned my world upside down. Everything was possible again. I wanted to sing and shout. I did shout – with pain.

We had hit an unexpected bump in the road. The Renault seemed to take off, falter, and come down in a belly-flop. I was jerked forward, then back. The seat-belt held me, but not my arm, which slid through its sling and banged against my injured ribs. Blackness.

'Jon! Jon! Are you all right?'

'Yes.' I struggled to keep myself on the surface of consciousness. 'I'm fine. But for God's sake don't drive so fast or we'll never get there.'

'We're not getting anywhere at the moment. We're parked.'

'I had noticed.' I laughed weakly. 'Carol, can I have a rest? Five minutes?'

'Sure.' She opened the car door. 'I'll take a walk.'

'No. I want to talk to you.'

'Okay.' She was reluctant, but she stayed.

I chose my words carefully. 'Carol, I believed you wanted a divorce and I provided the necessary evidence to make it quick and simple. I didn't have a girl-friend in Washington or anywhere else. From the time we met until I was posted to Oslo I never looked at another woman. I loved you and I wanted only you. If – if it matters to you, I still do.'

Carol looked at me. Disbelief, hope, joy, doubt walked across her face in quick succession. Her tongue came out and licked dry lips.

'But why – why, if you felt like that, did you accept what I said in a fit of temper? Didn't you realize how much I loved you? And there was Paul. He wouldn't even recognize you now.'

I didn't answer immediately. I didn't know what to say to her. I was torn between a feeling of extreme happiness and a desire to throttle Robert Verson. Verson had tricked me. He had told me Carol was disgusted by my supposed rape of Darlene Smith and wanted no more of me. He had lied. She

192

knew nothing about it. She hadn't judged me out of hand, as I had thought. And, if he had lied over that, what else had he lied over? Had he seized an opportunity to get rid of me or had he created the opportunity himself?

'There's more to it, isn't there, Jon?'

I was breathing fast. 'Yes. A hell of a lot more, but let it go for now. Please, Carol. I'll explain later. I promise.'

'Okay.' She didn't like it but she accepted it, and we got going again. 'But I'll hold you to that promise so don't try to wriggle out of it.'

'I won't.'

I grinned. It was wonderful to feel close to her again. But in forty minutes we would be in Dinard. Then there would be England, and Fel, and Verson, and a whole crop of problems. I settled down to think.

Parts of that night were seared on my memory for ever but other parts had grown vague over the years. Until recently I hadn't given it much thought. There had been the occasional horrendous nightmare, but otherwise I had adjusted to the situation, or what I believed to have been the situation – the Smiths had set me up in order to extort money from Fel. When Fel had told me at the conference that they had in fact got little out of it, I had been shaken, but I had told myself that Fel's idea of little was not mine and as long as the Smiths had been satisfied with only one payment he would have considered it fair, and not extortion. Anyway, I had had neither the opportunity nor the inclination to pursue that matter.

Now, because of what I had learned from Carol, it was different. I needed to rethink the whole thing, to look at it from a completely fresh point of view, to ask myself if Verson – and not the Smiths – had been initially responsible. It wasn't easy. I had to flog my brain.

I ended with a collection of suppositions. If Verson had some hold over the Smiths . . . If he had been able to make some open-ended arrangement with them, whereby as soon as he gave them a signal they would go into action . . . If he had been prepared to take the risk of framing Fel's son-in-law . . . If Fel had been prepared to turn a blind eye . . .

It was impossible to reach a clear-cut verdict, but neither could I rule out any of the suppositions. Verson had seen me storm out of the house that night. He had known the sort of mood I was in, and that it was an even bet I would make for the town and the pubs. He could easily have phoned Smith, told him I had taken the white Cadillac, and let him proceed with a plan they had already concocted. That Verson was capable of such behaviour I had no doubt. He was a ruthless character, used to getting what he wanted, and what he had always wanted was my wife. He had the best possible motive, and it was one with which Fel sympathized.

Altogether Verson made more sense than the Smiths, especially if the 'little' that Fel claimed they had gained was taken literally. And there was one other pointer that had always bothered me – the scent Darlene Smith had worn, which was Carol's favourite. If you get into the habit of buying a particular perfume you're apt to go on doing so even if the recipient isn't the same, and if Verson had wanted to give Darlene some small encouragement . . . I sighed. More 'ifs'.

Carol broke into my thoughts. 'Here we are, Jon. Dinard airport. You must be glad.'

'Yes.' I smiled at her. She had misinterpreted my sigh. But I was glad, very glad. It had been a hideously uncomfortable drive. 'What happens now?'

'There's a café upstairs. I'll show you. You wait there while I go and find the pilot and do some phoning. Have a whisky. You look as if you could do with one, Jon.'

'I'm okay.'

I said it as much to reassure myself as Carol. Now that I was out of the Renault I felt extraordinarily shaky, as if I had

194

just recovered from flu. I was sweating hard, my legs were like rubber and everything seemed slightly unreal. But I had to make an effort. I held out my hand for my overnight bag.

Carol gave it to me reluctantly. 'Are you sure you can manage?'

'Positive. I've only been poisoned, drugged and thrown down the cellar – ' I stopped short. This was no time to start telling my story.

'Christ!' Carol stared at me, her eyes enormous, her lips ajar, her forehead creased in astonishment.

She recovered before I did. I was still stammering when she snatched the bag away from me, seized me by the arm, led me into the building and sat me down on the nearest seat.

After that things happened fast. Dinard is a small airport and not the most luxurious in the world. At the moment it was busy. There was trouble. A flight to Guernsey was grounded with engine failure, its would-be passengers pregnant with enquiries. A party of Germans who believed themselves to have arrived at St Brieuc were lost and angry and demanding attention. The plane from Paris had just landed.

Nevertheless, within ten minutes I was installed in someone's private office. Beside me was a tray containing lemon tea – I had firmly refused the offer of whisky – and some quite presentable buttered toast. The pilot, a chap of about my own age but bursting with vitality, was found. Our passports were stamped, Customs waived, the Renault dealt with.

Carol wasn't Fel's daughter for nothing. She had a natural authority, she expected things to be done for her and she was good with people. Admittedly the English telephone operator thwarted her, but only temporarily; when she did get through and asked that we be met at Eastleigh, I had no doubt that on our arrival a car would be waiting. It was all very reassuring. I sat there, ate my toast, drank my tea and let everyone mill around me. I felt like an aged invalid.

I did balk when the pilot, who had come to collect us, offered me his arm. That was stretching the ridiculous too far. I was perfectly capable of walking out to the aircraft by myself. When Carol tucked her hand under my elbow, however, I raised no objections. I didn't object either when she helped me into my seat and found the belt for me. I just wondered what would happen to our new-found understanding when she was confronted with the stories of Darlene – and Anna. Because this time I was determined that Carol should be told everything.

The flight was uneventful. The formalities at Eastleigh were minimal. The car was waiting for us, though it wasn't the chauffeured Rolls I had expected. On the contrary it was a Mini, this year's model but badly dented. The driver was Lady Linden. The Rolls, she explained, had taken 'Lindy and that darling man Bob Verson to London'. Personally she loved her Mini Mouse and wouldn't drive anything else, but she would hate me to feel insulted.

Hurriedly I avoided Carol's eye. She hadn't warned me about Diana Linden. After five minutes I knew why. She was afraid I might have refused to come; and well I might. Anyone who could describe Robert F. Verson as 'that darling man' was no friend of mine and, as I soon discovered, Her Ladyship had other eccentricities. She never stopped talking and she drove the Mini as if it were a fire engine.

'. . . delighted to have Governor Felard. Lindy and I don't care how long he stays. As I told darling Carol here, we're honoured to have him. Such a splendid man. I mean, he's got everything, hasn't he? And so brave. Fancy risking his life to save that girl from the fire. I do admire – '

She broke off to wave at a motorist she had nearly forced into a ditch. 'Now why did he do that?' she asked in amazement as he shook his fist at her. 'He had plenty of room to pass.'

Carol, turning to share the joke with me, surprised the pain that contorted my face, and her grin faded. I tried to signal reassurance, but I was having a rough ride. My efforts to wedge myself into a corner had failed and there was nothing to hang on to except the edge of the seat. I was being banged around unmercifully in the back of the Mini.

'Well, everyone doesn't drive like you, Diana dear,' Carol said ambiguously, 'and it's a bumpy road. Very bumpy. Would you mind if we went a bit slower? I'm sure being jolted is bad for Jon's arm.'

'Of course. I was forgetting the invalid.' She slowed to thirty-five, which was quite fast enough considering that she insisted on hogging the middle of the road. 'And I was counting on you for tennis tomorrow, Jon. Lindy and Bob won't be back until the evening and we need a fourth. My brother will be disappointed if . . .'

She went on and on. I didn't listen. As the words flowed from her so the speed of the car increased, and I concentrated on not doing any more damage to myself than was unavoidable. Carol tried another protest but it was useless. I had to grin and bear it.

As a result I was once again exhausted when we drew up in a swirl of gravel in front of the Lindens' house, a hideous late-Victorian pile. I had to call on all my resources to get myself out of the Mini and stand upright. I leant against the car until the world stopped revolving. Nothing would silence the hammers that were beating on my skull; they even drowned Lady L's chatter.

'Jon, are you okay? Can you make it?'

'Sure, I'll make it.'

But it was a long way to go, up a flight of stone steps to the two leering lions which sat on either side of the front entrance. I was still struggling, with Carol's help, when the

197

front door was flung open and Fel came out. He showed surprise at my sling and my general feebleness, but no concern. He stood and waited for us. It didn't seem to occur to him that he might offer some assistance.

The last time I saw Fel he had been lying on the floor of his bedroom at the conference centre at Lysebu, a sick man. Verson's anxiety hadn't been feigned; he had been desperately worried about Fel – and not just about the Governor's image. To judge by appearances Verson could have no need to worry now. Fel, bronzed, relaxed, immaculate in a white dinner-jacket, radiated health. I almost caught myself looking for the cameras.

'. . . took us so long, but we've got here finally and what I want more than anything in the world is a real, honest-to-goodness American Martini.'

'I'll be mixing them the moment you give the word, Diana. But here, let me take those bags from you.'

Fel seized Carol's suitcase and my overnight bag. Lady L had carried them up the steps without any effort but it was a gallant gesture of Fel's, somewhat spoilt when he promptly passed them over to a manservant. He turned to me – Carol and I had just reached him – took my hand, and shook it with enthusiasm.

'Glad you could come, Jon.' He beamed at me; his teeth were very white against his tan. 'But what have you been doing to yourself? You look like the wrath of God.'

His handshake had hurt me and the happy, casual indifference of his words was infuriating. 'I've been fighting your bloody war,' I said, and my legs slowly folded beneath me.

'And what have you been doing to yourself?'

This time I didn't resent what was a formal question. The doctor proved to be highly efficient. He gave me a pain-killing injection in the shoulder. He strapped up my ribs. He bound my wrist, which he said must be X-rayed the next day.

He put a couple of stitches in my head. He was good and he showed no curiosity. Sitting up in a comfortable bed, in what I guessed was the Lindens' fourth or fifth best bedroom, I began to feel human again.

Supper came. There was cold consommé, chicken, salad, strawberries and cream, cheese – and a half-bottle of champagne. This was the life of Riley. I ate the lot. Carol brought the coffee herself.

'I told Dad he couldn't see you tonight unless you agreed, Jon. Don't you think it would be better to leave everything until the morning?'

It was a temptation and I was allowing myself to be tempted when there was a tap at the door and Fel came in. Carol expostulated, but he swept her objections aside. As usual, Fel intended to have his own way.

'We have important business to discuss and it's not going to do Jon any harm to talk for a while. So you leave us, sweetie, and we'll get on with it. I'm sure Jon doesn't mind.'

'And if he does, you'll mention Darlene and he'll do whatever you say, Dad?'

Fel's mouth stretched into a smile but his eyes were hard. He looked at me speculatively. The atmosphere was charged. Carol, who had stood up angrily when her father came into the room, sat down again and purposefully crossed her long, slim legs.

'You don't mean you want him back, Carol?' Fel said. 'After what he's done?'

'What has he done?'

'Didn't he tell you? Committed rape! This Darlene Smith. Your ex-husband raped her. He says he didn't but that's because he was so drunk he doesn't remember. He raped a girl!'

I heard Carol catch her breath and anger welled in me. Fel had been deliberately cruel. There had been no need to fling the lie at her like that or to phrase it so that my denial would be worthless.

'Two girls,' I said. 'Aren't you forgetting Anna, Fel?'

'Anna.' Fel hesitated. 'You admit it? You tried to rape Anna?'

I grinned savagely. I had surprised him into betraying his doubts. And now I understood why he needed to talk to me so urgently. In spite of – or perhaps because of – my supposed rape of Darlene, Fel had distrusted Anna's story, and it was imperative that he should know the truth. Because if Anna had lied to him, as he suspected, if Anna wasn't to be trusted . . .

'Who the hell is Anna?' Carol demanded.

Neither of us paid any attention. Fel was staring at me as if he were trying to bore into my mind. It didn't worry me. I propped myself up higher on the pillows and returned his stare.

'If one, why not two, Fel?'

'Jon, I warn you. I want the truth and I intend to get it if I have to beat it out of you.'

I had come here to tell him the truth. I had no choice. I couldn't let the East Germans' conspiracy succeed. It wasn't only Fel and his wretched image that were at risk. But I was going to make him sweat for it.

I said: 'I swear to you that I have never raped anyone, attempted to rape anyone or had any desire to rape anyone. However, since you chose to disbelieve me about Darlene Smith, you're obviously in something of a quandary. You've got to decide, Fel. Are you or are you not prepared to believe me about Anna?'

I could almost hear his brain clicking over, weighing the pros and cons. I didn't for a moment doubt that in his heart he knew me to be innocent on both counts, but to admit it was another matter. It made him either a fool or a knave over Darlene. And then there was Verson, whom he'd sent to London on some errand to get him out of the way. What

200

would Verson's reaction be to my declared innocence? Fel was an astute man, but he was having to juggle a lot of balls in the air.

And suddenly it didn't matter on which side Fel came down. Carol had put her hand over mine and was gripping it hard. That was all I wanted. She believed me. She didn't need proof.

'Okay. When I get back home I'll look into it. Talk to Darlene and her husband myself,' Fel drawled.

I didn't suggest he might have done this before, and not left everything to Verson. There was no need to spell it out for him. I stifled a yawn. I was beginning to feel sleepy. I didn't say thank you either.

I said: 'But you must know about Anna at once? All right. I'll put you out of your misery. At least you'll be sure where you stand. But first, Fel, when Anna telephoned you, did she say she was staying with a Madame Lesage near Paris?'

'Yes, but how – how could you know – ?'

I didn't bother to hide my bitter amusement. 'Anna told me what she was going to do before she left me for dead in the cellar of my house in Brittany.' I grinned at him. 'Sorry to sound so dramatic, but . . .'

I made the story as brief and factual as possible. Tiredness had caught up with me. I could barely finish what I had to tell them. My eyelids were drooping.

'The bitch, the goddam bitch!' Fel said viciously.

'Well, you can tell her to go to hell now.' I couldn't stop yawning. 'Even the propaganda value of poor dead Gerda and her beautiful daughter isn't worth much in the circumstances. Once the East Germans know I'm alive and their nasty little conspiracy is blown, what can they do?'

It was a rhetorical question and I didn't expect an answer. I remember Carol arranging my pillows and helping me to lie down. Then I was asleep. I didn't know I had asked the wrong question.

Chapter Seven

BREAKFAST WAS BROUGHT to me in bed and afterwards I bathed, shaved and dressed. It was a slow process but, apart from my wrist which affected the whole of my arm and an occasional stab in the ribs if I breathed too deeply, I was back to normal. I went downstairs to find Carol.

There was no one about except for a foreign maid and I failed to communicate with her. I wandered around the rooms that I hadn't seen the night before. I noticed some fine pieces of furniture, a beautiful Chinese rug in the drawing-room, and half a dozen interesting modern paintings. But I wasn't here to make an appraisal of the furnishings. I went out on to the terrace.

In the distance there was the put-put of tennis balls, voices calling, a burst of laughter. Following the sounds I came to the court. Lady Linden was playing singles against a man who was obviously her brother. I had to wait until the end of the game before I was introduced and could ask for Carol.

'Carol's gone up to town. She left with her father right after breakfast. I offered to drive them. I thought I might pop in to Wimbledon. We've tickets for Friday and – '

I interrupted rudely. 'Fel's taken Carol to London! Why?'

'I really don't know, Jon. I never asked them.' Lady L's smile was sweet, but her voice was tart and for once she was succinct. 'Not my business.'

202

Her brother – his name was Peter Kerr – was more sympathetic. 'They'll be back late in the afternoon.' He grinned at me. 'Actually, I don't think Carol wanted to go, but you know what the Governor's like.'

I did indeed, to my sorrow. And I wondered what the hell he was up to now. Why should he suddenly dash off to London, and take Carol with him? The next thing would be they had both returned to the States, and it would be no consolation that Carol mightn't have wanted to go. If Fel decreed, Carol would obey. Nothing had changed. I fought with my disappointment.

'Incidentally,' Kerr continued, 'they're expecting you at our local hospital about twelve. I'll drive you over as soon as I've changed.'

'Thanks. I'm sorry to be a nuisance.' At least it would help to occupy the day. 'Is it far?'

The hospital was ten miles away, mostly along country lanes, and I was grateful for Kerr's circumspect driving. We talked mainly about the States, where he had relations and where he travelled regularly on business. He was surprisingly well informed, especially about Fel for whom he seemed to share his sister's enthusiasm.

'He's a great man, or could be. Trouble is, he's not a household name, not yet. But that can be remedied. He's beginning to build. The World Environment Conference got him plenty of publicity the other side. It's a popular cause and of course rescuing that girl from the fire was absolutely super. There's still plenty of time before the elections.'

'What?' My attention had wandered.

'The Primaries. He'll need to put up a good show in quite a few of them. Of course, he could be a Favourite Son any time he liked, but that won't get him the nomination.'

'Nomination? You mean a Presidential Nomination? Fel? You must be joking.'

'I'm most certainly not. The Americans could do a lot

203

worse than Max Felard for President, at any rate in my humble opinion.'

Kerr had spoken coldly, and I didn't want to offend him. I said, 'A lot worse, yes. I'm sure you're right.'

I didn't sound very convincing, even to myself, and Kerr opened his mouth as if to say more, but changed his mind. He waved a well-manicured hand at me.

'We're almost there. On your left, the red brick building. That's the hospital. Diana's laid everything on for you. I hope it works.'

To my surprise, it did. That is if his cryptic remark meant that I should be treated with courtesy and efficiency. My experience of the National Health Service was more or less nil and I hadn't expected such consideration. I commented on our way back.

Kerr grinned. 'The name of Linden works magic in these parts. Lindy was their MP for fifteen years before he was elevated to the peerage, and a damned good MP too. I always knew he'd make it to the top. I'm good at picking winners.'

I nodded, but carefully avoided comment. It was obvious he was referring to Fel and, though his suggestion that my ex-father-in-law might be thinking of trying for a Presidential Nomination was astonishing, and in present circumstances absurd, I didn't want to get involved in an argument. I turned the conversation to the nice, safe subject of Wimbledon.

This lasted us until we reached the house, through lunch, and during the afternoon while we watched play on the box. For once Lady L didn't chatter. She and Kerr were both absorbed. Personally I found it hard to concentrate. My thoughts kept turning to Carol, Fel, Verson, and as the hours crept by it became more and more difficult to feign an interest in the tennis.

It was half past five when I heard a car on the gravel of the driveway. Regardless of match point I got up and went to the window. Fel was just getting out of the Rolls, followed by a florid man in his mid-forties whom I assumed to be Lord Linden. There was no sign of Verson, or Carol.

Feeling murderous I let myself out of the room and made for the front door. If Fel had played some clever trick . . . But Carol was hurrying along the corridor, as pleased to see me as I was to see her. She had dropped Fel at the Lindens' town house and spent the day by herself shopping. She hadn't seen Bob Verson at all. Fel had told her he had gone to Paris.

Paris? Why? The explanation had to wait. Fel had gone to his room and was not to be disturbed before dinner. I spent the time pleasurably, walking around the grounds with Carol, catching up as best we could on our years of separation. The one thing we didn't discuss was the future. It seemed to be a subject we both wanted to avoid.

After dinner I took much the same walk with Fel and, as soon as we were clear of the house, he began without preamble. 'Jon, I've told Bob Verson about Anna.'

'You have? I thought you didn't want to.'

'I didn't, but I decided it was inevitable. Needless to say, he was horrified. But he couldn't have been more understanding.' Fel put his hand on my shoulder; he was laying on all his charm. 'Bob's prepared to help, Jon – in any way he can.'

'Good.' It was an inadequate response, but I was getting a whole range of warning vibrations.

'He's already gone to Paris. He's going to get in touch with Anna and arrange a meeting, where he'll lay everything on the line. I'd like you to fly over tomorrow morning and join him, Jon.'

'No. Nothing doing.' It was a definite refusal. 'I'm sorry, Fel, but I've done enough.'

'You have. Of course you have, and I couldn't be more grateful. I'll make it up to you, Jon. I swear it. But I need you to go. Don't you realize what a difference your just being there will make?'

'You mean, if I confront her, there's no argument. She knows the conspiracy's blown and that's that.'

I said it reluctantly. Fel had a point. All the same I was loath to go to Paris. It wasn't that I was scared the East Germans might make another attempt to kill me. They would have nothing to gain by it now. Indeed, once they were aware that I had survived their previous efforts and there was no longer any hope of planting Anna on an unsuspecting Fel, I was sure they would abandon the whole scheme. They really had little choice. But I still didn't want to go to Paris.

'You'll do it then, Jon? I can count on you?'

I hesitated. 'Fel, I – ' An idea had occurred to me. 'Yes. All right. I'll go.'

'You will? That's splendid.'

He didn't bother to ask me why I had suddenly changed my mind. He delved into his wallet and, to my amusement, produced an air ticket and a stack of francs which he passed to me.

'Here you are, Jon. The Lindens' chauffeur will drive you up to Heathrow in the morning. You're booked on the twelve o'clock flight. That way you can lunch on the plane and be free for whatever Bob may have set up for the afternoon. I hope he'll be in touch with Anna by then.'

'Where do Verson and I meet?'

'He'll be waiting for you at the airport – at Charles de Gaulle. If by any chance you miss him there, he's staying at the Georges V. Which reminds me, he had difficulty getting a room – Paris is very full – and we never arranged anything for you.'

'It's not necessary.' I was quick. I had no desire to stay in

206

the same hotel as Verson. 'I have cousins in the 16th *Arrondissement*. They'll put me up.'

'Great. I think that's all then, Jon.' He gave me his friendliest smile; he had never doubted I would eventually agree to go, but he was pleased I had given in without a fuss. 'With luck everything should be okay.'

The next morning I sat in the back of the Rolls and thought about what Fel had said. He was right. With luck everything should be okay, except that for me everything included recovering the passport I had processed for Anna. And that was going to take a hell of a lot of luck.

Still, there was a chance. It was when I realized this that I had changed my mind about going to Paris. It was a very slender chance but, whatever the odds against, I had to take it. If only I could get that passport back I should be safe again. There would be no need to make up some stupid lie for H.E. about being infatuated with the East German girl, no possibility of prosecution, no dismissal from the FCO. And with my career intact, I could ask Carol if she would remarry me.

For a while I daydreamed happily. Then reality got in the way. I had no idea what arrangements Verson had made with Anna, where or in what circumstances we were to meet her. As for the passport, Verson had no knowledge of its existence; I had said nothing about it to Fel. It was just possible Anna might bring it with her to our meeting. And if so . . . I blew out a sigh and hurt my cracked ribs. Probably the bloody passport was already being inspected by some communist official in East Germany.

The chauffeur had pushed aside the glass partition that separated us. 'Which terminal, sir?'

'Two. Air France.'

'Very good, sir.'

I hoped it would all be very good, but I doubted it.

Heathrow, which is my least favourite airport, was as usual chaotic. There were too many people, too few seats, too many empty beer mugs and half-eaten sandwiches, too few urinals, too many frayed tempers. I was thankful when my flight was called and we boarded the plane.

It was an Airbus, and the first-class compartment was a third empty. I was one of the lucky ones and had no one sitting beside me. The lunch was excellent. The champagne was unlimited. It was a pity I couldn't make the most of such unaccustomed luxury but I was too much on edge to enjoy myself. And the nearer we got to Paris the more tense I became.

Yet everything was going according to plan. The aircraft landed on time, neither Immigration nor Customs delayed me, and Verson was waiting near the agreed exit. He greeted me affably and led me along the concourse to a bank of lifts.

'You've eaten, Jon?'

'Yes, on the plane.'

'That's great. I've an automobile in the carpark. We can get going right away.'

'Where to?'

'To the village where the lady's living.'

'You've made contact with her, then?'

'Sure. I've arranged to meet with her this afternoon. She thinks it's to be a preliminary discussion of the logistics of getting her to the States, but hopefully it'll be a final meeting, very final.'

As if this were some kind of joke Verson threw back his head and laughed loudly so that the people standing around us in the lift stared at him. It gave me an excellent view of the inside of his mouth and the new dental work he had needed as a result of his fight in the tunnel at the conference centre. The sight cheered me. At least he hadn't got out of this business scot-free.

'I see you've had your teeth fixed,' I said unkindly as we went in search of the car.

He gave me a baleful glance. 'Yeah. Temporarily. The rest will have to wait till I get home. Ah, here's our transport. I nearly didn't recognize it.'

That seemed to amuse him, too, though I failed to appreciate the joke; there must have been thousands of four-door beige-coloured Citroëns in Paris, similar to the one he had rented. He was in an odd mood. I told myself to watch it.

I said, 'Before we go, tell me briefly. When you spoke to Anna on the phone, what were your impressions?'

'She was word-perfect. If I'd not known the truth I'd have accepted her for what she's supposed to be. My God, when I think – of course Fel had promised he would send someone, so she was expecting a call.'

'From you?'

'Not specifically, but she remembers me from the conference at Lysebu. She knows I'm close to Fel, and that gives her confidence.'

'Did you talk for long?'

'About five minutes. The theory is that Madame Lesage, for whom she's meant to be doing some temporary house-keeping job, plays bridge every afternoon, and Anna's free from two-thirty on. That's what she told Fel. I called at the appropriate time and she answered the phone. I avoided names but I made it clear who I was, and she agreed we'd meet today. It was as simple as that.'

'It sounds all right.'

'Not to worry, Jon.' Verson started the car and backed out of the parking space. 'There's no reason on earth why she should have been suspicious of me. And I'm an optimist. I've got every hope of finalizing the matter this afternoon.'

Grinning to himself – it could have been a nervous grin – he paid the parking attendant and drove out of the airport into the hot summer sunshine. The temperature was in the low eighties, probably two degrees higher than it had been in London, but the sky was overcast. I wound down the window to get some air, but there were only petrol fumes and the noise of the traffic. Conversation, if not breathing, was impossible. I wound up the window.

'Where exactly are we going?'

'To Mireil St Cloud. It's west of Paris, in commuter land, only a village, but with some nice homes on the outskirts. They're on the edge of the forest and they have big yards.'

'You've been there?' I showed my surprise.

'Sure, but not in this automobile. Small places are apt to be curious, though fortunately this one's used to foreigners.'

'How do you know that?'

'I heard some kids yelling to each other. They were Americans. I also noticed a couple of cars with CD plates.'

I nodded. 'That was smart of you.'

'I'm a smart guy, Jon. I believe in good organization, and that means taking every possible precaution beforehand.'

'Yes.' I smiled wryly, thinking of the business of Darlene Smith, though it was something I had promised myself to forget temporarily. 'And Eva – Madame Lesage – lives in one of these large houses.'

'It's the farthest from the village and the most isolated. I offered to call there while the Lesage woman was supposedly at her bridge. I guessed Anna would say no, and of course she did, on the pretext that Madame might return unexpectedly. But it was a show of good faith on my part.'

'Where are we meeting Anna, then?'

'In a lane that runs between the back of the house and the forest. I suggested we could either sit in the car and talk or go for a drive, and she agreed at once. It's an ideal arrangement, Jon.'

I grunted. I didn't like it, though I couldn't have said why. I hoped Verson wasn't being too confident. Anna wouldn't come to the rendezvous unprepared. She was more likely to have a gun in her bag than the passport I wanted. Then there was Eva, and others could be in the house, Günther and Horst perhaps. Someone could follow us. Not that it should matter if they did. I didn't know what I was worrying about.

'Not far now,' Verson said. He swung the Citroën off the main road and immediately took a sharp left turn, making me grateful for my plastered wrist and the professional strapping on my ribs. 'And we've plenty of time in hand.'

But minutes later he was swearing. Somewhere he had made a wrong turn. We were lost in a maze of little lanes. Angrily he slewed the car to the side of the road and pulled up. I watched while he pored over a map. I had to suppress my irritation. Time was ticking away. Then in the distance I heard the whistle of a train.

'Is Mireil St Cloud on the SNCF?'

'The what?'

'The railway. Does it have a station?'

'Yes. Why?'

'There was a signpost pointing to *la gare* about half a mile back.'

Without bothering to refold the map Verson thrust it inside the door pocket and jerked the car into reverse. He was, I realized, as tense as I was, though he relaxed a little when he got his bearings and recognized the road again. We drove past the station. But instead of going through the village as I had expected, he turned up the hill and came around behind. We were now on the edge of the forest.

Verson glanced at his watch. 'We've about twenty minutes, Jon. Let's go for a walk.'

'A walk?'

'Yes. You're fit enough, aren't you?'

He sounded quite solicitous and I had to remind myself that over the years something of Fel's behaviour would have rubbed off on him. 'I'm fine,' I said. In fact, physically I was

211

in better shape than I had hoped, but my nerves were taut.

'I want to have another look at the lane and the back of the house. I'll show you.'

I followed him, through the trees and along a narrow ride. The air was heavy and warm with insects. Verson walked fast. He seemed to have forgotten his former concern for me. He was almost surprised by my presence when I caught up with him.

'That's the house?'

'Yeah.' He swallowed. 'She'll come out of that gate there, and walk down the lane towards us. It's a deep lane, with a high wall on that side – they like their privacy around here – and a bank on this. No one will be able to see her, and if anything goes wrong . . .'

'For Christ's sake, why should it?' I interrupted his musing. He was more jittery than I was. 'If there's going to be trouble it'll be when she's faced with me. But when's that to be? You were priding yourself on your efficiency a while ago, yet you still haven't told me exactly what you intend us to do.'

Verson, apparently satisfied with what he had seen, was retracing his steps. 'You hide in the back of the car under a rug. It won't be too comfortable but you'll have to bear it. I pick up Anna and as soon as we're going fast enough so that she can't jump out I accuse her of being a communist agent. You appear like a jack-in-the-box. She realizes the game's up. And between us we put the fear of God into her. How's that for a scenario?'

'Well,' I said, 'she won't scare easily.'

'Won't she? Just you wait, Jon.'

'Besides, there's not much point in trying. We're never going to change her hatred of Fel or her desire for personal revenge. What we can do – what we must do – is make it bloody clear to her that the conspiracy has failed and there's not a hope in hell of blackmailing – '

'Jon! You play it my way. You understand?' Verson stopped, his hand on the car door. 'I didn't want you in on this. Fel insisted. But now you're here, you'll do as I say. I will not have you interfering.'

Verson spoke through thin lips. His eyes were hard, like blue marbles. And I was startled by his venom. There was a spot of spittle at the corner of his mouth.

'Cool it,' I said. I couldn't keep up with his changes of temper. 'You're forgetting we're on the same side – for the moment.'

'Okay. Get in.' It was an order.

I got in the back of the car and settled myself as best I could. Having an arm in a sling didn't make it easier. Verson arranged the rug over me. The Citroën had been parked in the shade but it was hot on the floor, stifling under the rug. I pushed it off my face. There would be plenty of time to cover myself.

Verson started the car and we edged forward. He drove quietly but down here I could feel every bump and rut in the road. It was worse when he turned into the lane and a relief when, after twenty yards or so, he stopped. I lifted my head cautiously.

The lane was bright with sunshine. As Anna came towards us, the sun would shine directly in her eyes and the back of the car where I half lay, half crouched, would be in deep shadow. The minutes passed. I shifted my position in an attempt to get more comfortable.

'Here she comes,' Verson muttered. 'Keep down.'

I heard the click of a gate. The engine was already running and we began to move. I had a fleeting impression of a green dress and long shining hair, then I was pulling the rug over my head. My heart thudded unevenly. The car gathered speed.

It can only have been moments before I realized something was wrong. Even so it was a gut reaction. I was still

213

struggling free of the rug when my mind took in what was happening.

Anna must have realized it seconds ahead of me. The car was roaring down the lane towards her and it wasn't going to stop. She jerked her head from side to side – the high wall, the steep bank. She turned and ran. She hadn't a hope. We hit her squarely and fractionally later I felt the sickening jolt as the back wheels went over her body. She didn't scream.

'Damn you! Damn you!' I was shaking Verson ineffectually with my one good hand. 'You've killed her. You did it on purpose.' I was shouting at him.

'Shut up!' He jammed his foot on the brake and I was thrown against the back of his seat. 'What do you think I meant to do, Troy? She's a goddam communist agent.' He was breathing hard. 'How can you have a United States President with a goddam commie for a bastard daughter?'

Chapter Eight

I HEARD WHAT Verson said but it didn't really impinge on me. By now I had the door open. Kicking my legs free of the rug I stumbled out of the car and nearly lost my balance. Then I was running down the lane to where Anna lay spreadeagled on her back. There was little doubt that she was dead but I had to make sure.

I fell to my knees beside her and looked into her face. It was contorted with fear but by some freak chance it had escaped injury. I stared at the honey-coloured skin, the wide cheekbones, the mouth I had kissed, and her green eyes stared sightlessly up at me. Her chest had been crushed. It was a mess of bone and blood, mixed with the material of her dress and strands of her pale hair.

The bile rose in my throat. I staggered to my feet. I had never loved Anna, but I had desired her. And she had been beautiful, too beautiful to be wantonly killed. That she had been completely indifferent to my own death was irrelevant. If I could have brought her back to life I would have done, regardless of the consequences. I didn't have the killer instinct.

But I did have some sense of self-preservation. I hadn't forgotten the passport – the main reason I was here. Verson had gone to the end of the lane to turn and was coming back. I was half surprised he hadn't driven straight on and left me. Certainly he wouldn't want to hang around longer than he had to. If I were to find that passport I must hurry. I slipped my arm out of its sling.

Anna had been carrying a shoulder bag. It had come undone and some of its contents – comb, lipstick, pen, change-purse – were scattered around her. The bag itself was wedged under her hip. Overcoming my aversion I lifted her and pulled it free.

The bag was one of those affairs with zippered compartments. The first contained a wallet, a handkerchief, a lighter and a packet of cigarettes. The second contained a gun. The last zipper stuck. My fingers were thumbs and there was blood on them. I wrenched the zipper open. In the third compartment was the British passport that could have put an ignominious end to all my hopes. Thrusting it into the inner pocket of my jacket I felt weak with relief, and stupidly grateful to Anna.

I was getting to my feet, the bag still in my hand, as Verson drove up. He was fifteen to twenty yards away and I remember the thought crossed my mind that his wheels would go over Anna's body again. The roar of the engine warned me. Verson was accelerating. He was driving straight at me. He intended to kill me as he had killed Anna. I was rigid with fear.

Like Anna I looked from side to side, seeking a means of escape. The bank was steep and offered no holds. The wall was over six feet high. Unlike Anna I didn't turn and run. I had seen what happened to her. To run was to die.

My one chance was to out-think and surprise Verson. But I couldn't even see him properly. He appeared only as a dark figure crouched over the wheel of the car. I must have imagined his face twisted with hatred, his mouth in a rictus. Fighting down my panic, I forced myself to wait. It was a long second.

Then the point came when I could wait no longer. The Citroën was closing on me fast. I could almost feel the heat of its engine as I drew back my arm and with all my strength hurled Anna's bag at Verson's head. What with the gun and the coins the bag was heavy, not heavy enough to break the windscreen, but heavy enough to startle Verson. And it was big. I hadn't done up the zips and things flew out of it. Momentarily Verson was driving blind.

At the same time I was leaping for the wall. Anna wouldn't have had a hope, but I'm six feet tall. I got my good arm over the top and began to pull myself up. But my left hand could do no more than scrabble at the stone and, as my body swung outwards, the car struck me. It knocked me back flat against the wall, tearing loose my hold. I slid to the ground. And there was a gap in time before I realized I was unhurt.

The car had roared past. I watched it hit the wall – so close to me I felt the shudder of the impact – and run parallel, gouging its side against the masonry. Then inexplicably it slewed across the lane at an angle of forty-five degrees.

Verson must have lost control. He was a good driver but he had been travelling too fast and in a confined space when his vision was blanked by Anna's bag. There was nothing he could do. The car mounted the bank, stood poised for a moment on its rear wheels and slowly turned over to crash down on to its roof.

The noise of crumpling metal and breaking glass sounded horrendous. I expected people to come running through their gardens and out of their back gates to see what had happened, but no one came. The noise subsided. The dust settled. The sun shone peacefully on the scene of carnage.

I must have been suffering from shock because I still didn't move. I stayed where I was, crouched in the lee of the wall, for another full minute. Even then it required a lot of courage to stand up, to skirt Anna's body – carefully averting my eyes for Verson had driven over her again and the sight was appalling – and get to the car. I peered in through the glassless window.

Verson was hanging upside-down in his seat-belt. He seemed to be standing on his head, and his head seemed to have been pushed into his trunk so that he no longer had a neck. His eyes bulged. His tongue protruded from his mouth. He was never going to have that expensive dental work he had promised himself. I felt sick.

Suddenly I became aware of the stench of petrol and, simultaneously, of the racing engine. I put my arm through the window and tried to reach the ignition key but Verson was in the way. I tried to move him but that too was impossible. And I wasn't going to stay to be killed. I began to run.

I was about thirty yards up the lane when there was a great whoosh of sound behind me as the petrol tank exploded. I turned to see flame and smoke billowing into the blue sky. Bits of metal flew around. One piece landed not far from me. I started to run again. If the crash itself hadn't attracted attention, the fire certainly would.

I ran until I was sobbing for breath. By now I had reached the top of the lane and turned on to a road that led through the forest. Here there was no bank and I was able to walk in among the trees. I sat on the ground. I was shaking uncontrollably. Then my stomach revolted and I unhad the champagne, the fillet steak, all the expensive lunch I had eaten on the aircraft a thousand days ago. I moved deeper into the forest. I rested with my back against a tree. And after a while my mind reasserted itself.

Standing up, I took stock of my appearance. I removed the sling that was still hanging round my neck and wiped my face and hands on it before stuffing it into a trouser pocket. I dusted down my suit. The toes of my shoes were scuffed from scrabbling at the wall but there was nothing I could do about that. I ran my fingers through my hair. I was now as ordinary, as much part of the local environment as I could hope to be.

I walked out of the forest, past the top of the lane and

down the hill. Luckily I've a good sense of direction. I had no difficulty in finding the station. It was on the other side of the market square and I was crossing over to it when I heard the distant but imperative klaxon of a fire engine. I thought of the blaze the Citroën had made, of Verson's incinerated body, of Anna. For no reason, except that I wanted to get as far from this place as I could and as fast as possible, I broke into a run.

At this time of the afternoon Mireil St Cloud was waking up after its siesta. The little shops clustered around the market square were reopening. Already a few housewives with their shopping baskets were beginning to converge on them. I felt curious eyes follow me as I ran. Deliberately I slowed my pace. I couldn't afford to draw attention to myself.

In the station I had to wait while a couple of boys, Germans with rucksacks, argued about their tickets, and when it came to my turn the chap at the *guichet* barely glanced at me. I went out on to the platform. The last thing I wanted now was to have to hang around and I was reassured by the sight of half a dozen people. Obviously a train was expected.

It came five minutes later. The passengers were mostly French, but there was a sprinkling of tourists. I was unremarkable. I took the nearest window seat and stared out at the passing countryside. I had a lot to exercise my mind.

So much, in fact, that before I had thought through half the implications of what had happened we were gliding into the Gare St Lazare. I made straight for the station bar. My top priority was a double Scotch. I let the barman add only a splash of soda so that the whisky was almost neat, and it hit my stomach with a marvellous, comforting warmth. Remembering that I was spending Fel's francs I nearly ordered another but decided, albeit reluctantly, that it might not be wise.

From St Lazare I took a taxi out to the airport. It was the rush hour. Traffic was heavy and it was a long, frustrating drive. I went straight to the British Airways desk. I had missed a plane by five minutes; their next flight was fully booked. I tried Air France. They had one first-class seat, leaving in three-quarters of an hour. I grabbed it.

Going through emigration I had a bad moment. I nearly offered Anna's phoney passport to be stamped instead of my own. I was sweating as the officer waved me on. I went directly to the toilets. I wasn't going to make the same mistake twice.

But it's not as easy to destroy a British passport as one may think. The paper is tough and the cover is hard. With little strength in my left hand I had the greatest difficulty in pulling out the pages and tearing them into pieces small enough to flush down the pan. The cover defeated me completely, until I thought of buying a pair of nail-scissors at one of the shops on the concourse and distributing the bits in various litter bins. Now, even if there was a fuss about the disappearance of a blank passport I could be as po-faced as anyone at the Embassy.

It was an enormous relief and I should have felt exultant, but in fact I was exhausted. Fatigue and pain – my whole arm was giving me hell – had suddenly caught up with me. I yearned to lie down on one of the airport's orange banquettes and sleep. But the day wasn't done yet. I telephoned the Lindens and asked to be met at Heathrow.

Because of the difference between French and English time it was only seven-thirty when the Rolls deposited me at the Lindens' house. The manservant who opened the front door informed me that the family were by the swimming-pool but he believed both Governor Felard and Mrs Troy were upstairs.

I tried Carol's room first. When she wasn't there I went

along to Fel's; he had a suite: bedroom, bathroom, dressing-room, sitting-room. I found the two of them together and my immediate impression was that I had interrupted a private conversation. Carol's colour was high. I didn't apologize.

Fel greeted me warmly. 'Come in, Jon. Come in. I wasn't expecting you until tomorrow at earliest, but when you phoned – ' He left the sentence unfinished and waved his hand towards a tray of drinks. 'Help yourself. Then come and fill us in on what's been happening.'

'Thanks.' I poured myself a modest Scotch.

Carol said, 'Before you start, there's something I have to say, Jon.'

'Sweetie, can't that wait? We've more important – '

'No, Dad.' She turned to me, ignoring Fel. 'Jon, I was just telling Dad, when your leave comes to an end I want to go back with you to Oslo. We can get a bigger apartment and bring Paul over and maybe, if you're willing, after a while we might get married again. What – what do you think?'

I grinned to hide the depth of my feelings. 'Darling, you forestalled me. I was going to ask you myself.'

'For Chrissakes!' Fel said. 'You ought to have more sense, Carol. Jon doesn't understand the position I'm presently in but – '

'What position?' I interrupted him. 'If you're talking about your determination to become the next United States President, Fel, I'm fully aware of it – now. Peter Kerr mentioned your hopes and Verson confirmed them. It explained quite a lot. Why the East Germans were prepared to make such a big, no-effort-spared production of planting Anna on you. Why Boris Gronski was at the conference at Lysebu; presumably the Russians were a party to the conspiracy and Gronski was sent to hold a watching brief. And why Herr Schreiber was so anxious about rumours of a communist plot to destroy you. He must have known, too.' I paused. I was watching Fel carefully. 'It also explains why Anna had to die.'

221

'Anna's dead?' Fel said slowly; his face was a blank, but the knuckles of the hand that gripped his glass were white.

'Verson killed her. He drove his car at her.'

'Drove his car at her? Deliberately?' Carol was shocked. 'Oh, no! Why? Once she knew you were alive and the plot had failed – '

Fel held up his hand. 'Let him tell it, Carol.' His voice was hoarse.

'Yes. It was deliberate, all planned carefully in advance. When I met Verson at the airport he was on a high with the excitement of what he was about to do. I should have realized it but I didn't. As to why, Anna hated Fel's guts because of the way he'd treated her mother. She wanted personal revenge. She'd always have been a menace.'

'But, dear God!' Carol was white.

Fel got up and poured himself another drink. 'Where's Bob at the moment? Why didn't he come back with you?'

'Verson is dead too.'

'What?'

And now I had shaken Fel. Anna's death had jolted him, but this was of a different order. Through the years his dependence on Verson had been great, as confidant, as prospective son-in-law, as hatchet man. I was sure Fel was no more directly responsible for Anna's murder than he had been for the Darlene Smith affair; Verson had acted on his own. Otherwise, surely, Fel would never have suggested my trip to Paris. Or had he intended to implicate me in whatever Verson might do? I would never really know. Fel was a devious man.

Even while I told them how Verson had died I could see his brain ticking over. How dangerous was the situation? Could it be saved, turned to his advantage? The explosion of the Citroën's petrol tank and the fire would have destroyed almost all evidence, but sooner or later Verson would be identified. The French police were good. He would need to have a story ready . . .

'It's tragic,' he said, shaking his leonine head. 'Tragic. Poor Bob. He must have been insane. Goddammit, but I'll sure miss him, especially in the campaign.'

I gazed at him in disbelief. It was incredible, but Fel, knowing how vulnerable, how open to blackmail he would be, was nevertheless prepared to put everything at risk to satisfy his ambitions.

'Fel, there's not going to be a campaign,' I said quietly. 'There's no way you can be permitted to become a candidate, let alone President.'

'And who's to stop me? You?'

'Yes,' I said. 'If you make me, I'll see that the British Ambassador in Washington is told the whole story, and he'll pass it on.'

Fel laughed without mirth. 'Don't be a fool! Carol, tell him not to be a goddam fool. Tell him what it means to be President of the United States, the greatest man in the greatest country. Tell him what it would mean to Paul, to all the family. He doesn't understand.'

For half a minute I doubted her. I thought that as always in the past she was going to side with her father. But she didn't.

She said, 'Dad, Jon is right. It's you who don't understand. You can cover up your heart trouble, as long as it's only minor, with stories of overwork and smoke inhalation, but this is different. There's no possibility now you could ever be President. Too many people – enemies of the United States – know about Gerda and Anna. Think what pressures they could bring to bear on you if you were elected. And when you didn't give in to them, think of the appalling scandal there'd be and what that would do to the States, the Presidency, the Party, all of us! There'd be rumours, gossip, perhaps even the suggestion that you yourself had – had organized Anna's death. You can't risk it, Dad. You – '

'Be quiet, damn you!'

Fel, beside himself with rage, had leapt to his feet. For one ghastly moment I thought he was going to strike her and I made to get between them. He was cursing and blaspheming. Then suddenly he faltered. One hand scrabbled at the front of his shirt. He fought for breath and, though we tried to support him, he collapsed on the floor. He died two hours later.

In many ways he was a great man, but he was ruthless, used to getting what he wanted. If he had decided to go ahead and seek the Presidency, would I have had the courage to carry out my threat to stop him? And what would Carol have done if I had destroyed her father? Thankfully we would never know now. The danger that yesterday's betrayal of an insignificant German girl could lead to tomorrow's treason was no more.